PROGRESS
AND
PERSISTENCE

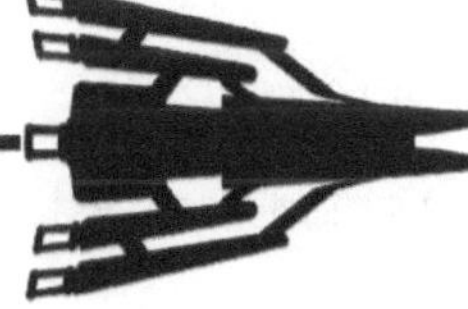

A.M. ACCETTA

PROGRESS AND PERSISTENCE

THE
GHOST OF
ARCTURUS

HAILEY SVARTHOLD

Consciousness. Existence. Being. Whatever she wanted to call it, Hailey felt it all at once. The familiar feeling of She couldn't feel anything; not technically. Her surroundings were black. Noiseless, colorless, neither warm nor cold. Hailey wasn't hungry, thirsty or tired.

In a way, she had asked for this. Hailey didn't know what the end result would be, but she wanted to do it all the same. Now, the afterlife was here; everything and nothing. She could float forever, finally at peace.

Hailey took stock of everything she could account for. *I still have my memories*, she thought. She tried looking down at her hands, but she couldn't find them. Only a still black void. *I have no body, no senses, but I can still think? Is this the afterlife? After everything I've heard about it, is this all it boils down to?*

A light appeared in front of her. Glowing white and flashing, a small rectangle appeared and disappeared in her vision, slow and repeating. Hailey tried to call out, but she couldn't speak. *What the hell is this?* An uneasy feeling set in as she realized what it looked like. A text prompt, waiting for input.

-Initialize

The word scrolled into frame and paused as if waiting for a response. Unease shifted to panic. *WHAT THE FUCK IS THIS? A program? Am I in a computer? Is **this** the afterlife?* She could almost feel every neural pathway light up trying to make sense of what she was seeing. The program responded.

-Initializing Bootup Sequence

These letters scrolled faster than the previous line. From that, Hailey could infer that the first line was hand-typed.

-Booting Binaural Microphone

"Doctor, I still don't know if this is a good idea." Hailey could hear a woman's voice. "The tech hasn't been tested well enough. We could lose the engram entirely."

"I know the risks, please keep conversation to critical updates and data," a man's voice sounded off in response, irritated.

The woman let out a sigh, "Well, her neural patterns went from nominal to off the chart as soon as we turned her ears on."

"She can hear us?" a second man asked, surprised.

"Of course," the first man responded. "What did you think *Binaural Microphone* meant? Hailey, if you can hear me, I want you to try and stay calm. This will be frightening to you, but everything will be ok." He tried to sound reassuring, but it only made Hailey feel worse. *Who is this person? These people? Am I actually dead, or did I botch the job?*

-Booting Ocular Array

NO, NO, NO!

Artifacts and pixels were all she could see, but Hailey could tell that the images were buffering. Slowly, shapes started becoming clearer. Lights, brighter. Space, closer.

She could see walls, grey and sterile. She could see people, masked in medical equipment, staring at her. *I can't move.* Hailey tried to feel for arms and legs, to grasp and kick, but felt nothing.

"Charts are not looking good. We may need to resume this at another time. The engram could fracture from the stress she's feeling," the woman said with urgency to the man in charge.

"How bad is it?"

"If she had a heart, it would've gone into cardiac arrest."

"Damn it, don't say it like that."

"You asked."

IF I HAD A HEART?! WHERE'S MY FUCKING HEART?!

"We can't shut it down. Her engram isn't likely to spin back up if we turn it off now. It's now or never."

"I'm getting an alert that a POL ship has entered atmo," the second man alerted the team. "They're looking for us. We have a day if we're lucky, hours if not."

"Do not stop now," a deadly serious tone carried the leader's words in a way that caused the other two to fall silent. Hailey could see them continue to monitor the situation.

-Booting Extra-sensory Array
-Terminate Extra-sensory Array
-Terminating Boot Sequence of Extra-Sensory Array

"Why did you stop ESA?" the woman asked.

"Normal senses are probably more than she's capable of coping with right now. If she wants, she can boot up ESA later. Hailey, I'm going to turn your voice on now. I know that this is stressful, but please try to stay calm and don't scream."

-Initialize Vocal Monitor

The placating tone of his voice sounded familiar to Hailey, but with everything happening at once, she didn't have the capacity to think about it.

-Booting Vocal Monitor

Hailey screamed setting free all the anguish and fear that she could muster as soon as her voice returned.

"WHAT DID YOU DO TO ME?"

"Volume control, *now*," the man in charge barked at the woman. The second man stood in the back as still as stone.

"Where the fuck am I? Why can't I move?" Hailey yelled as loud as before, but the output was smaller, quieter. Her voice sounded tinny and sharp.

"Hailey, please, calm down."

"How do you know who I am? CALM DOWN?! WHO ARE YOU?"

The man pulled off his mask and showed his face. A face that Hailey hadn't seen in years. Crow's feet and greying temples marring a face she once looked up to so long ago. "It's me, love. It's Dad."

————

Three hours later, Henry paced a small room painted stark grey with a bed against the wall. In his peripheral vision sat an android named Hailey. His dead daughter occupied its framework.

Hailey could sense her father's trepidation. "You haven't even thought about what you'd do if you got this far, have you?" Henry continued to pace, giving her a slight glance as a response. Hailey stood and kicked the bed, denting the steel with surprising ease. Henry turned to face her.

"Hailey, please. Stop. I know this is a lot, but I—"

"You have no idea what *any* of this is like!" she yelled. Hailey stilled as she came to a sudden realization. "No one knows what this is like. I'm the first, aren't I?" Henry said nothing, but his eyes told her every truth she needed to hear. "You finally got the engram to work, then."

"Love, I couldn't stand it. I had to do something."

"What did I tell you? Didn't I tell you that the paladins wouldn't let you keep researching this? Now that they're planetside, what do you think they'll do when they see me? They hunt and kill any AI. Even if we get away from them today, you've set me down a path that has me running for as long as this body remains operational." Hailey looked down at her 'fingers.' Five thick, articulating wires combining to form a palm, hauntingly similar to a human's muscular structure.

"You are not an AI," Henry responded dryly.

"The Paladins of the Order of the Lesser are a religious order and you played God. They don't like that."

"That's on me, then. I can give myself up to the POL and make a deal. I'm guilty, not you."

"What if I'd prefer that they kill me?" Henry heard Hailey's words but stared at her blankly.

"I don't follow."

"Did you even look into how I died?"

"Hailey, we have the family legacy to think about here. The Svartholds are extremely important to galactic political structure. We need you."

"I killed myself, Henry." Whether it was the outright confession or her referring to her father by his first name, Hailey couldn't be sure, but she knew it hurt him. "How could you do this to me? Do you have any regard for my choices? Do you love me – *your daughter* – or your legacy?" She wanted to cry but couldn't.

"I gave up everything for this. I can never return to academia, let alone ruling the Outer Reach. How could you ask if I love you?"

A knock rang at the door. Henry opened it.

"I'm sorry to interrupt, but we need to start packing up to leave." Henry's assistant, Clara, was at the door. Hailey recognized that she was the woman's voice she heard during bootup. "David's drones have caught sight of the POL in town."

"Understood. Give us another five minutes, please."

Still getting used to her body, Hailey awkwardly walked past them through the door. "No need."

"Hailey, wait- "

"No, I'm walking into town and giving myself over to the paladins."

"You can't do that! They'll- "

"Fuck you, '*I can't*.' I made my choice." She waved them off and continued to walk down the hallway.

"HAILEY! Damn it, they won't kill you. If they take you, it'll be worse than death."

Hailey stopped in the hall. She could hear the motors in her legs whir to a halt. "How do you know?"

HENRY SVARTHOLD

In his prime, Henry was the foremost scientist in the field of the human mind. He found it fascinating that even after humanity conquered the galaxy and mastered faster-than-light travel, they still could not fully understand the brain and, more importantly, consciousness. To be something in this universe, wherein more than 99% was empty space, seemed improbable. To be sentient on top of that, seemed impossible. He had built his science around a single question: Is the human experience quantifiable?

This question, in Henry's mind, needed a mathematician as well as a philosopher. Henry spent many nights enraptured by this question, though he rarely had time to pursue his hypotheses.

The emperor had named the Svarthold family a great house after the destruction of AI for their part in the war. Had Linda Svarthold not investigated a strange sequence of code in a seemingly ordinary briefing, reality may have come apart completely. As of now, reality had only bent and separated at the seams because of the war with the AI, an event that had come to be known as The Shattering. Almost a thousand years later, the Svartholds still held the throne of the Outer Reach.

As Lord of the Outer Reach, Henry Svarthold had many responsibilities that took him away from his research: coordinating the greater and lesser houses of his territory and earning their fealty, placating the native species in the sector while also prioritizing human interests, and simply keeping his people fed.

In his heart, he was an academic and a scientist. He gave years of his life to the duty of rule but would spend any free time he had studying the conscious mind. *Do we have the mental capability to understand what it is to be conscious? Can we boil down the human experience to an equation? Is mathematics the language that can convey these ideologies?* Henry could find no better place to be than in the expanse of his own mind, constantly asking himself these kinds of questions.

Henry held court, listening to the concerns of his constituents. In the great hall sat his throne at the end of a long, white stone room, flanked by tall windows. The throne was made of a type of marble native to the Svarthold throneworld of Arcturus, which was dark grey with veins of orange spiderwebbed throughout. When the light shone in from the windows, the veins of orange glowed. Despite its beauty and craftsmanship, Henry felt a throne was ostentatious, and rarely used it. He preferred instead to hold court at a large table to speak to his people eye to eye.

"My lord, we have only one more appointment."

"Any details?" Henry asked Sir Gerard, the captain of his personal guard.

"Sir, this one is strange." Gerard was an imposing man, but more approachable than most royal guards. Jovial with a protective nature. This is why Henry liked having him as his personal guard and captain. Gerard's demeanor changed, however, upon relating the information of the next appointment. Looking at his tablet, he said, "It's a Paladin of the Order of the Lesser."

This took Henry by surprise. "Does it say why they're here?"

"No, my lord."

"Well, show him in, then."

"Yes, my lord."

While Gerard left to gather the paladin, a child entered the hall from a side door. She ran over to Henry with a toy.

"Dad, look!" The child had programmed a simple hologram to fly out of her hand like a bird.

Already on edge, Henry snapped, "Hailey, I told you, I am holding court. Go to your room or bother one of the serving girls. Leave, now." Hailey had left, slumped and defeated. The holographic bird flickered and disappeared.

Gerard returned and announced a man larger than the already large captain of the Svarthold house guard. "Sir Alan of house Harbrand, Paladin of the Order of the Lesser." The man stood six and a half feet tall, balding with a salt-and-pepper beard. Harbrand held a glaive in his right hand. He looked to be in his mid-fifties, but in relation to relative galactic time, he was several hundred years old.

Members of house Harbrand were referred to as immortals in galactic courts. This was disingenuous, however; Harbrand's throneworld, Hoard, revolved around a black hole and suffered from time dilation. Their own lives passed in normal time by their perception, but the galaxy around them was on fast-forward. The extreme gravity of their planet caused an extreme environment and, in turn, extreme peoples. Humans native to Hoard were tall and extremely strong, with steadfast beliefs and tenacious resolve.

"Lord Svarthold, thank you for receiving me. Arcturus is just as beautiful as I remember it." Sir Alan Harbrand's baritone voice clashed against the stone walls, as though it were too big for its surroundings.

"Sir Alan, welcome to Arcturus and to my home. Please, take a seat. Forgive me, but I'm surprised by your visit. The Core is far and the Void farther. What brings you to the Outer Reach?"

He took a seat at the table across from Henry, leaning his glaive against an empty chair. A thin, red banner hung near the blade, emblazoned by the sigil of house Harbrand: a wave crashing against stone, black and white against a red backdrop.

"My lord, I hope this discussion does not come across in a negative manner. I'm aware the Svartholds and the Harbrands have not always been friendly in years past, but I'm here only regarding the Order."

"Of course." Henry was familiar with the Harbrand family's tendency to hold grudges. The fact that time progressed slower for them only exacerbated it. "Is there some sort of illegal arcane practice taking place on Arcturus? My police would be happy to work with you in order to bring them to justice."

"No, my lord. I come only to speak, not to make any attempt at justice. It's regarding you and your research."

Henry had never had a poker face. He could tell his reaction was being read like a pamphlet by Harbrand. "I don't understand," he said, trying to keep his voice from shaking, "my research is only on the human mind. I thought the Order only sought artificial intelligence and illegal forms of the arcane."

"That is a common misconception about the Order. Do you know what the '*Lesser*' refers to in our title?"

Henry shook his head, "I admit, I don't."

"The term '*Lesser*' refers to all of us. You and I. The emperor, the commonfolk. Humans as well as all other sentient species. The Order is based in Agnosticism. We believe that all of us are lesser than. To what are we lesser, we cannot know by our own design. The Order of the Lesser is pious in its humility, and we strive to keep humanity from destroying itself as it almost did in the war with the hive mind. The most destructive force is our own hubris."

"I'm sorry, but I'm still confused. What does that have to do with my research?"

Harbrand retrieved a small tablet from within his cloak, tapped the screen a few times and showed the screen to Henry. "This is your patent for, what you call, a consciousness matrix engram, is that correct?" Henry nodded and looked at Harbrand. Though solemn, there was a slight sparkle in his eyes. Henry knew why; a Harbrand was putting a Svarthold to question. He had the emperor's blessing and was loving this. "Can you tell me what this does?"

"It's only theoretical. My attempt at quantifying human intelligence and consciousness into an engram that can be saved and archived. I haven't been able to get the math to work."

"I see." Harbrand slipped the tablet back into his cloak. "I hope you understand why this may be of interest to the Order."

"I'm afraid I don't."

"With this technology, if it were to exist, one could theoretically bring someone back from the dead. This rides a dangerously fine line with what our order considers forbidden. If someone were to be revived, the order would be forced to imprison them for the rest of their days. That could mean eternity given the circumstances of your technology's longevity. We wouldn't kill them, as they're not technically artificial, unless we *absolutely* had to."

"Longevity is exactly the problem," Henry rebutted. "They may live longer than a normal human would, but the engram is likely to decay over time. If it was not properly maintained, that could mean decades, maybe centuries, of slowly going insane. If you captured someone in these circumstances and held them in perpetuity, the anguish they would feel would be immeasurable."

"It would be my humble suggestion to never finish this work, then."

Henry felt his heart sink. "But this is my life's work."

Harbrand stood and grabbed his glaive. "I must take my leave, but I will leave you with this reminder from the Order and the Emperor." Towering over Henry Svarthold, Sir Alan Harbrand had warned him, "You are not a god, you are lesser."

SIMON CANSBY

"This is Persistence, requesting launch from Trebuchet Aquila." Bill, the captain of the Persistence, sat in a swiveling flight chair suspended by a mechanical arm from the ceiling of the ship. The Persistence was a corsair class ship; swift, yet versatile. It housed a kitchen area commonly referred to as the "mess", two bedrooms, and a small living area for entertainment. The starboard corridor was for observation, with narrow windows at eye-level running the length of the ship, whilst the port corridor had reinforced walls and hidden doors, held basic medical supplies and an armoury, and was known as the Citadel. Simon knew that the Citadel was Bill's pride and joy with its inbuilt fail-safes.

Simon had been through a trebuchet a few times now, but the process enamored him. Sitting in a passenger flight chair next to his mentor, Sir Alan Harbrand, he soaked up every detail.

"Corsair Persistence, this is Trebuchet Aquila. Please transmit verification codes and throw coordinates," a voice responded on the comm speaker.

Bill tapped a screen with his right hand and held down a button for the microphone with his left. "Transmitting now."

"Standby."

Bill was gruff. Mutton chops adorned the sides of his face like the banners that Simon and Harbrand flew from their glaives. Persistence was Bill's ship, but it had been in the employment of the Order for a couple of years. During this time, Simon had never seen Bill without his trucker cap. An artifact of old humanity, this cap had a plastic mesh on the back and sides. The front was stained and faded white with an image of a bear. Below the bear read, '*California Republic*.' *If this thing were new, it'd probably be worth more than my ship*, Bill had drunkenly told Simon one evening. Simon knew of Bill's proclivity for exaggeration and was skeptical; he had never heard of California before.

The comm speaker crackled and came to life once again. "Persistence, you are clear for travel from Trebuchet Aquila to Trebuchet Hastings, Outer Arm. Travel time is four days, eleven hours and forty-four minutes."

"Copy, Aquila. Beginning approach." Bill slowly moved Persistence toward the trebuchet. Trebuchets were often considered as the invention that won humanity the cosmos, though many years had passed since their initial installation. Now, the Empire of Humanity was so reliant on these gates that it was a part of their culture, galaxy-wide. Hundreds now dotted the eight sectors of the empire, throwing ships large and small at so fast a pace that nothing was out of reach. Everything passed through a trebuchet: food, goods, passengers and anything the empire needed to keep churning. Journeys once thought of as life-fulfilling odysseys had become a commute.

The trebuchet was a large ring, seventeen miles wide in diameter, with control towers stationed perpendicularly every mile. Once inside the center, a space-time bubble would form into a sphere around the ship and "throw" it into the cosmos. When Simon first observed a ship sent through a trebuchet, he was reminded of a simple bubble wand from his youth. A thin screen of soap stretched across the ends of an empty ring. When you blew into it, it would convex, stretching until it reached a breaking point and separated from the ring, creating a bubble. This looked similar to the effects the trebuchet displayed when creating, and separating from, a space-time bubble.

As Persistence approached the breach, Simon felt the pull of artificial gravity wear off. From the range of windows, he could see electricity arcing from the control towers to the ship.

"Persistence ready for launch," Bill called over the comm.

"Godspeed, Persistence. Going superluminal in 3...2...1..."

This was Simon's favorite part.

Many argued that superluminal travel wasn't possible, and the process only created an alternate reality where the traveler was already at the place they wanted to be. Although proven incorrect, it was hard to argue this logic when looking out of the window during a throw. Some said it looked like the spacecraft was slipping through the bonds of this dimension, breaking reality. Simon simply thought it looked like an ocean. Every color the universe had in its myriad - nebulas, gas clouds and stars - blended into a single blue-white hue. It glowed through the windows, occasionally flashing streaks of orange, red or purple. Simon could stare for hours, adrift in his own mind, like someone watching a campfire.

"Let's recap the mission." Harbrand turned to Simon and said, "Target?"

"We've received intelligence that the rogue scientist and traitor Henry Svarthold is hiding in the outer arm. We're to check the Barcelona system, specifically planet B-115 for any signs."

"Good, I can see that you've been studying your mission reports."

"Thank you, sir." Simon felt a sense of satisfaction at this remark. Praise from Alan Harbrand was few and far between. "I do have a question, though. Isn't this the planet where practitioners of the Book of the Swarm reside?"

"Yes and no," Harbrand responded with a cool resolve. "The Order had found them there about 15 years ago, Relative Galactic Time. We traveled in force, myself included, and eradicated them. That said, some survivors are likely, but I don't think they are arrogant enough to have stayed. We shouldn't run into any of them."

"What was it like to fight them? I've only heard bits and pieces of what their magic actually consists of."

"We try not to use the term '*magic*' – '*the arcane*' is a much broader term that encompasses this as well as fringe science and new physics that came after the Shattering."

"Right, I'll be sure to use that in the future." Simon made a mental note and continued, "If you don't mind me pressing, though, what was it like? To fight the Book of the Swarm, I mean."

Harbrand stared into the middle distance for a moment, seemingly editing his thoughts for removal of painful memories while thinking of a summary answer to the question. "It wasn't easy. We lost a few exceptional men and women of the Order that day.

"The practitioners worked in the field of particles, believing that each and every particle has a mind of its own. Through ritual drug use and haphazard use of a particle reactor, they were able to make contact. Since then, they were able to communicate with their deity by hallucinating and sacrificing living tissue to allow the swarm to grow and reproduce. The cost of their sacrifices continued to grow. Starting with plant life, graduating to small animals, and eventually sentient children, both human and non-human alike.

"We don't know what the swarm was actually made of. It seems unlikely that it was made of particles, as those are far too small to make any physical change in the world, but there was always a hungry cloud of nano... things that would, well, *swarm* around you and feed."

"How were you able to defeat a cloud of sentient particles?"

"We had our own practitioners. Members of a prestigious university on my planet that studied the arcane field of gravitation. This was, and still is, a legal form of the arcane. They conjured gravity wells that helped to hold the swarms at bay while the Order slew the men guiding them.

"Once we had control of the swarms, we brought them into the vacuum of space and released them. The radiation annihilated them almost instantly."

"What happened to the occultists?"

"I slew their leader myself. I never knew his name; he and his followers referred to him as *The Magistrate.* With their leader killed, most fled and we put others under arrest to face the emperor's justice."

Simon was enthralled. This was why he joined the paladins. There was so much evil in the universe, and it was always humans that created the evil. Simon held the acolyte's oath in his heart stronger than any words could ever promise.

"Four days will be enough time for some rest, I think." Harbrand unbuckled his seatbelts and grunted as he stood up. He put a massive hand on Simon's shoulder. "Dismissed, Acolyte Cansby."

"Yes, sir. Until we're called upon."

"Until we're called upon," Harbrand replied to the verbal salute of the paladins and turned away. He ducked through a door frame and disappeared into his room. Simon continued to stare out the window past Bill, until he drifted to sleep.

HAILEY SVARTHOLD

"Corsair class," David, Henry's assistant, told the party while staring through binoculars at the paladin's ship grounded next to a distant town. "These things are fast. If we get into orbit, there's no way we can outrun it. On top of that, this looks like a private contractor. Who knows what kind of aftermarket upgrades the pilot has installed." David looked away from the binoculars and back at the group, waiting for a plan of action.

The party consisted of Henry Svarthold, Clara Brightwater, David Hill, a Carthian everyone called Hopper, and Hailey herself, all seated upon a short ridgeline outside of town. Hailey wore a desert veil with a mesh to cover her alloy face. This planet, wherever this planet was, had an arid climate, so the veil wasn't out of place. The party, however, was like a palm tree in a snowfield. Henry Svarthold was well known galaxy-wide. The Brightwaters and Hills were Svarthold Bannermen. Why they were here, Hailey still couldn't discern. It seemed strange that they would give up their lands and titles; if they were being chased by the Order, they were considered traitors.

Carthians were native to the Inner Reach but were frequent visitors to Arcturus and the Outer Reach. Smaller than humans, only about four-and-a-half feet tall on average, they had spindly limbs, arms that almost touched the ground, with two fingers and a thumb on each hand. They had eyes on the sides of their heads, indicating that they evolved as a prey species, and dull blue skin. Carthians were known for their ability to communicate telepathically at short distances to both sentient and non-sentient life-forms, giving them a reputation as nature guides. Hopper wore a helmet from his home world made of an iridescent metal, with a plate on the front that came down between the eyes.

Hailey looked at Hopper and realised a wall had been put up between them. She may be sentient, but she was technically a machine. Hopper couldn't talk to her. "How does a Carthian get caught up in this?" Hailey asked aloud. Hopper's right eye focused on her. She could tell that Hopper was trying to say something, but all she saw was his gaze; all she heard was the wind, until Henry spoke.

"You'll make your way over to the ship and no one will know you've left," he commanded the crew. Their own ship was a simple freight carrier. Sub-light class, meaning it was a smaller freight carrier, and very common throughout the galaxy.

His confidence took Hailey by surprise. "That sounds suspiciously like you've formulated a plan," she said with an air of sarcasm to her father. Henry turned and gave her a sardonic look that quickly shifted to a quiet sadness, like he'd forgotten what he had done to his daughter.

"I do, but it won't be pretty." Though he spoke with a dry tone, Hailey could hear an edge of distress. He looked at his watch and said, "We have about another hour or so."

While sitting atop the rough ridgeline at the edge of town, Hailey had time to think. It was a strange feeling; she couldn't be sure if they were even *her* thoughts or a reflection in code. How could anyone take her seriously when that question was sitting there unanswered?

Hopper looked at her like he could tell what she was thinking, but Hailey remembered that Carthians were a very empathetic species, so he was likely just giving her situation some thought. She had seen a few in her time at court as she grew up. The thought of home and court brought a problem to mind.

"You said I was important to political structure," she turned to Henry, breaking the silence. "How could you expect that I would ever be taken seriously in galactic court like this?" She gestured broadly at her body.

"I don't know, Hailey," Henry responded in a low tone.

"You don't know?"

"I don't. Please, I'm sorry. I'll do everything I can; explain whatever you want once we're out of here."

"Not even a stray thought to the future and what that might look like for me?"

"Hailey, I was destroyed when I heard you were gone. I don't—"

"Just raw instinct?"

"Hailey, I—"

"*We'll just bring her back!*" Hailey interrupted with a heavily sarcastic tone, waving her arms satirically. *"The emperor will love that! All hail Hailey Svarthold, Lady of the Outer Reach, Botcher of Suicides.* How could I even—"

"I DON'T KNOW!" Henry screamed, his eyes welling with tears. Silence penetrated the group for too long a moment before he choked out, "I may be intelligent, but

I've never been wise." Tears ran down the length of his nose before falling to the dry, dusty ground.

Hailey shifted closer and leaned in. In a grave tone she reminded Henry, "I want you to think about the tears you're shedding right now and remember that I can't do that anymore."

Henry began to sob softly. Hailey was hoping to feel some level of vindication by hurting him. She *wanted* to hurt him. She instead felt empty while watching him break apart. The group tried to give them space but couldn't move too far on the short ridgeline, and they drowned in the moment.

Hailey stood and walked a few paces, turned and looked at the rest of the group. "Well, we have one plan, at least. Go on. Enlighten us, Henry. How are we supposed to get away from the Order?"

Henry regained his composure and wiped his eyes with a dusty sleeve. "Fine," he said, defeated. He stood and faced Hailey. "It's not like you could be any angrier with me. You asked me if you were the first. You aren't. You're the second."

Hailey felt a cold distress. "What did you do?"

Henry took a moment and a breath, then replied, "I made a deal with a devil."

HENRY SVARTHOLD

Henry stood over the computer and stared at the screen. Every wire double-checked; every line of code sifted through. A moment of apprehension had seized him. *If I hit* Enter, *there is no coming back*, he thought. *If I stop now, I can apologize and swear fealty to the emperor. I can name a successor to the Outer Reach and move forward in academia. Just so long as I stop now.*

Henry stood over a humanoid metal body. Motionless, it lay on the medical table. He had procured it from another planet in the Barcelona system called Argon.

Trade in these types of bodies were considered illegal, but it was the soft, grey kind of illegal. Most law enforcement really didn't care if anyone owned one, unless they were trying to add charges to their rap sheet.

Henry had wandered the streets of Eclipse, Argon's capital city, feeling more alien than the non-human entities that dotted the hustle and bustle of the lower streets. He had asked numerous vendors for full-array humanoid drones. Only when he was about to give up, he found a back-alley bartender with the goods he wanted.

Henry stood over it all. In a stark grey room outside of a small town on B-115 in the Barcelona system, he stood over one of these humanoid drones. He stood over the computer that could bring them to life. He stood over his feet; a surprising reminder of just how human he was. *I can stop now. It's not too late.* He looked to a shelf in the room six feet away. Upon it sat a hypercube, about the size of his thumbnail. Within was an engram. Within was everything he had taken for granted; a love he couldn't recognize until it was gone. Within was something far too large for its boundaries. Henry felt no less anxious but was nonetheless reminded of his dedication upon looking at the cube.

Henry hit *Enter.*

-Initialize

A few minutes later, after programs had booted and senses returned to the entity in front of him, Henry asked plainly, "Zachary, can you hear me?"

There was a painful pause before the vocal monitor kicked in and responded in a cryptic manner, "Nobody calls me that."

"Well, nobody calls you *anything* anymore," Henry told the android. "You've been revived into an artificial body."

"How long have I been... down?" The voice almost sounded groggy, though this was likely Henry's cognitive bias.

"Fifteen years."

Zachary was silent for long enough to make Henry wonder if the engram had shut off. While he was checking the screen, the android spoke again. "Who are you? Why am I here?"

"Simply put, I am a man in a predicament. I need an insurance policy, and I think we have a common interest. I take it that you're familiar with Sir Alan Harbrand, correct?"

The neural activity display that Henry was monitoring blossomed after this question, but the body was silent. Another painful pause passed before Zachary responded, "Quite."

"You're here because I need protection. There's a ship that will need to leave the planet soon. Harbrand will be an obstacle; but he's the reason I revived *you* in particular."

Zachary found agency of his neck and turned his head slightly to Henry. "What are you offering?"

"Revenge."

SIMON CANSBY

Kick. Simon looked around when he felt the thought ring out in his head. He saw a pair of Carthian children looking at him in the town square. Between the two of them and Simon was a wooden ball sitting in the dirt.

Kick? He felt it again and realized it was one of the children. He didn't hear it in his head; communication from Carthians was *felt.* An image from Simon's youth, playing sports with his brothers, flashed for a split second, as if the child had sorted through his mind like a filing cabinet and pulled the closest approximation to what he was trying to communicate. Simon understood the Carthian children wanted him to kick the ball back to them.

With a wry smile, he fulfilled the request. He kicked the ball to the children, and one stopped it gently with his foot. Simon was shown feelings of joy and gratitude in his mind, then the children turned with the ball and continued to play.

"I'll have you know, if you're harboring fugitives," Harbrand was standing in a nearby door frame speaking to someone inside, "it's considered high treason against the empire. I trust I don't need to educate you of the consequences." He turned with a huff and stepped back into the town square towards Simon.

Calling this assortment of buildings a town was generous. A dozen sand-brown adobo-style houses ringed an open courtyard, creating a loose town square with multi-colored cloth stretched from rooftops and poles driven into the dirt. Proprietors sold goods and necessities from these ramshackle kiosks below the tapestries. Simon occasionally caught the scent of toasted spices through the constant smell of hot dust.

As Harbrand approached, Simon noticed that eyes were staring at them from every corner of the market. He wasn't surprised. Simon guessed that these people had never seen a Paladin of the Order in-person before. There was another element in their gaze, however, that left Simon feeling anxious. He couldn't place it, but he felt that they were experiencing more than just quiet intimidation from the presence of the paladins.

"I don't know where this man could be," Harbrand's voice sliced through the dry air. "My intuition tells me that these people know more than they're letting on, but we're getting stonewalled."

"I feel it too, sir," Simon confided. "I saw outlying buildings a few miles out when Bill and I surveyed during touchdown. Should we try those?"

Harbrand shifted his glaive from one hand to both and stared into the distance outside of town. Simon followed his gaze and saw four individuals slowly making their way toward town. Simon readied his glaive in response, and they began walking silently toward the group.

They met in the open a few dozen yards from town. Harbrand and Simon stood like sentinels, their dark-grey cloaks billowing lazily behind them, while waiting for the group to make the last leg of the approach. Underneath their cloaks, they wore top of the line mark IV Phaistos plate armor made of ceramic nano-weave. Along with their glaives, that also served as gauss rifles, they had energy field emitters attached to their left forearms. These emitters were known as the Shield of the Lesser.

As though named in a call-and-response manner, their glaives were referred to as the Arm of the Greater. This pair of tools constituted the symbol of a paladin's duty; shield the Lesser, and carry out the clandestine will of the Greater.

Two women, one man and a Carthian approached through the desert haze. *Another Carthian?* Simon thought. The Carthian, wearing an iridescent helmet, must have sensed Simon's thoughts and turned to look at him. There was no response from the little blue entity, but he felt a bleed of emotion emanate from that stare like he was trying to mask his feelings. *Anticipation?* Simon considered what that could mean when one of the women spoke.

"Sirs, we came as soon as we heard the Order was planetside." Simon recognized the grammar and speech patterns the dark-haired woman had. She seemed to be more educated than the townsfolk. "There's a scientist performing sadistic experiments in the plains beyond the ridgeline." She pointed out behind them. The other woman had covered her face with a veil and remained silent.

"Thank you for coming to us," Harbrand responded. "Is there anything you can tell us about this scientist?"

"I'm afraid we don't know much, sir," the young man chimed in. "We operate the radar array about a mile from here."

"What can you tell us of the experiments?"

"It seemed like the scientist was bringing people back to life in android bodies."

How could they know that level of detail about it? Simon thought. Then he felt *fear*. Not from himself but projected from the Carthian. Then *regret*.

"Is that him?" Harbrand pointed with his chin behind them. A few hundred yards away, two men were walking toward town. "Thank you for your assistance here today. All of you should get to cover. Please let the people in town know that they should remain in their homes until this situation is resolved."

The four left without saying another word, but Simon took one more look at the Carthian with the helmet. Their eyes met, *guilt*, but only for a moment before he turned and left with his companions.

After walking the open sands for a few minutes, they stood face-to-face with Henry Svarthold. Dishevelled and dirty, with tears drying on his cheeks, Henry was the ghost of the Lord of Arcturus. Beside him stood an android. Though the sight of the two was strange, Simon couldn't help but think about the Carthian.

"Henry Svarthold," Harbrand called out in an authoritative voice, "by imperial law and by the emperor's decree, I place you and your companion under arrest." *Anticipation, fear.* "I hope the two of you will surrender peacefully." *Regret, guilt.*

Something wasn't right. Simon couldn't *stop* thinking about the Carthian.

"Alan, I knew that you'd be the one to find me," Henry said in a tired, gravelly voice. "In fact, you were always there, waiting for the Svartholds to misstep." *Anticipation, fear.*

"I've always known the Svartholds aren't the benevolent leaders they pretend to be, Henry."

"Confirmation bias, as we scientists call it. Your family has always been angry that you lost the territory skirmishes. You wanted us to be evil to make it easier to justify your hatred." *Regret, guilt. What did the Carthian do to feel guilty? Does he know something he never let on?*

"This would wound me if you weren't a known fugitive standing next to your own criminal evidence. Who is this... entity?"

Fear, guilt, regret, anticipation. What was he anticipating? Why was he anxious? Simon's eyes widened as the pieces fell into place. A trap.

"An old friend of yours."

Simon's hands tightened around his glaive as the android's voice sounded off, "You killed me, paladin." Henry's tears began flowing once again. *Fear, anticipation.* Simon was feeling his own, now.

"Who are you?" Harbrand commanded.

"The Magistrate," the android responded, slowly raising his arms.

The last anyone ever saw of Henry Svarthold was right there when he dropped to his knees in the dust. He muttered something Simon couldn't make out, before bursting into a cloud. A *Swarm.*

IN THE SHADOW OF ECLIPSE

HAILEY SVARTHOLD

The group ran immediately after the paladins turned their attention to Henry Svarthold and the Magistrate; past the market with its watchful eyes, past the low hills in the open desert and the corsair Persistence. The spaceport on B-115 was that in name only, with little more than markings on the ground that indicated where to land, made diminutive by the Persistence. It loomed over the unassuming Progress in the open field.

They loaded up onto the Progress and buckled in, except for Hailey, who stopped at the airlock, looked back and saw her father melt into a swarm. The paladins began swinging wildly. The swarm hit the larger one, giving the younger one a chance to fire off the gauss weapon in his glaive. Clara pulled her onto the ship by the arm, threw her into a chair and closed the airlock.

Hailey couldn't move. She never wanted any of this. She was heartbroken and furious at the same time. It was *her* decision. He robbed her of that and made it *his*. There was no regard for her choices, only a grief-stricken decision to rewrite history. *I could have at least told him that despite everything, I loved him*, she thought. She wasn't sure if it would have been a lie, but it would have been comforting to him before he died. The guilt set in.

When they finally reached orbit, Clara had gathered herself and approached Hailey. "I'm not even going to try and pretend like I know how you're feeling. I'm sorry, truly, for doing this. I genuinely thought I was doing my part for fealty to house Svarthold and honor for the Brightwaters, but after everything, I'm not sure."

"I don't really want to talk to anyone." Hailey was blank. She wasn't sure if she had reached her mental capacity, or the limits of the android's processing power had been capped out. Somehow, she felt tired, but knew she would never sleep again.

"I don't blame you," Clara responded. "We're going to get out of the system and lie low. We'll have plenty of time to talk if you need that. David and I are going to discuss next steps, but we could all use a break." Clara waited for a response but wasn't surprised when none came. "Let me know if you need anything."

I need to get drunk, Hailey thought. *I'm back from the dead. What the hell am I going to do now?*

SIMON CANSBY

"I'M GOING TO KILL EVERY LAST ONE OF THEM!" Harbrand screamed while Simon did his best to stop the bleeding. Missing his left hand, Harbrand writhed on the dinner table aboard the Persistence. Tendrils of bone and muscle coalesced upward from the missing hand to eventually meet halfway up the forearm. He had reflexively used his shield in an attempt to stop the swarm. This was the first part of him they began to devour. Unprepared to deal with the threat, he could only swing wildly while his arm was being shorn. "EVERY ONE OF THE BASTARDS IN THE VILLAGE. AGGHH! THEY ALL KNEW!"

Simon was able to snap a shot off with his glaive's internal gauss rifle, shearing the Magistrate's alloy head off at the neck. After the controller was gone, the swarm slowly dissipated, but the damage was done. His left hand and half of his forearm was missing, apart from some ribbons of flesh and sharp needles of bone that remained; shadows of the arm that was there moments before. Once the threat was gone, they made their way to the ship. Simon noticed a small shipping carrier take off from nearby the Persistence as they were making their way back. *It must be those people who came to see us,* he thought, *the group with the Carthian.*

"Bill!" Simon called out from the mess hall to the cockpit. "We need to get to orbit, now! Find somewhere with emergency medical!" Simon felt the Persistence rumble beneath him almost immediately. The core under his feet spooled up and rocked the ship back and forth gently while the mercury fuselage increased rotational speed. It stabilized, and they were afloat.

"We're going to Argon!" Bill yelled back from the cockpit. "Fifteen minutes!"

Argon, the capital planet in the Barcelona system, was known for housing every flavor of organized crime. Drug, slave and weapon trade operated in the shrouded and crowded streets of its cities. Primary among these cities was Eclipse; the largest and most densely populated metropolis on Argon. Eclipse was a layered city in both literal and metaphorical terms; many levels of streets teeming with art and crime in equal measure.

Even though crime was a part of everyday culture on Argon, the melting pot of human and non-human cultures created a robust economy centred on the arts. Food, media, music, paintings, theatre; Argon had some of the best the galaxy had to offer. Surprisingly, the cartels of Argon had been good about establishing and paying local taxes, creating a debate around the good that can be created from evil. The cartels thought in terms of business longevity: if people want to stick around, you'll have more customers. Make Argon a more lucrative place to be as a normal citizen and business will be cheaper and easier to sustain. Simon was still unsure just how much of this was true to everyday citizens and felt that proponents of the benefits of a necessary evil likely were only the ones that benefited from it.

"It took my shield," Harbrand muttered after he had calmed a little. "It was my first one since becoming a paladin." He shifted his eyes from his injury to Simon. "Emperor Desmond VII bestowed it upon me after swearing my oath."

Simon didn't know that about Harbrand's history. When Simon swore his oath, it was to the Prime Cardinal of the Church of Scholars. To swear your oath to the emperor is a great honor; Simon understood why he was so heartbroken.

Fifteen long minutes had passed before they finally reached Argon's orbit.

"This is corsair Persistence requesting an emergency landing. We have a Paladin of the Order that needs immediate medical treatment," Bill hailed.

After 10 seconds had passed with no response, Bill hailed again. "Persistence to Eclipse Transit Command, *do you copy?* Request for *emergency* medical landing, this is for a *Paladin* of the *ORDER*. How copy?" A few more seconds trailed on in silence. Bill inhaled to try again, but just before he could broadcast, the monitor came crackling to life.

"Corsair Persistence, this is ETC. We copy." The man spoke in sputters and stops. It sounded like he wasn't sure what he was doing on the other end. "We uhh... we can get you a spot."

"*...alright? AND?*"

'Roger, Persistence, please proceed to... uhhh... Bay 34, Harbor 7, mid-level. We'll have medical meet you."

"Copy, ETC," Bill responded aggressively. "Persistence in-transit." Bill slapped the module to shut the broadcast off. "For fuck's sake." This would normally be a time that Simon would smile and pat Bill on the back, but he was elbow deep in Harbrand's blood.

Persistence began flying in between the different levels of Eclipse, passing large corporate buildings, haphazard hovels and every class of atmo-capable ship known throughout the Outer Arm. They touched down on the landing pad in Bay 34, Harbor 7, along the edge of one of the common areas, known as walkabouts, that meandered through the city connecting pedestrians to the businesses, restaurants and ship bays throughout the honeycombed labyrinth of Eclipse.

As soon as the landing gear was planted, the doors opened. Simon saw a daunting tumult in front of them. Every color of light was shown through the walkabout; bright advertisements for Incledan Ramen, Harsuan White-Horn Skewers, and Thessian Surf-n-Turf. Simon even saw an entire sign on which the word '*CORN*' was emblazoned. Other kinds of businesses threw their colors into the damp city air, including several that advertised cornucopias of adult services, both human and non-human alike.

He tried to help Harbrand down the short ramp, but the man's sheer size made that impossible. They were met by a medical team and the ETC representative that spoke to them during the landing request. He looked terrified.

"My lords, we are humbled by your visit." He shuffled sideways to let the medical team pass. As they began to escort Harbrand, the ETC rep spoke again, "I'm confused, is there no med bay aboard the ship? This seems like it could have been taken care of in—" He was interrupted by a strike from Harbrand's right hand as he passed, sending him crumpling to the ground.

Simon broke off from Harbrand's escort to help the man back to his feet. "Sorry about that," he said, and once firmly planted, Simon began to brush dirt and oil off the

ETC rep. "He can be quick to temper. We were attacked by dark practitioners. We need to run checks on his wounds to be assured there won't be any lingering damage and our med bay isn't equipped to handle that." The rep seemed dazed, but overall ok. "I'm Simon."

"Me..." The man blinked vacantly before regaining his faculties. "Timmett. I'm Timmett. Let me know if I can be of any more assistance." He left without another word. Simon fell in step and followed Harbrand.

EDGAR THRAWL

Just a few more steps, Edgar thought as he skulked from behind the corner of the alleyway. Edgar felt his synapse response notify him of the text.

I'm here.

Come in, babe, I'm waiting for you ;)

He peeked around the corner, seeing a short, hooded man approach a darkened door in the alleyway. Edgar was relieved to learn that all his targets were here on Argon, most with apartments in Eclipse. The hard part was luring them out. Killing them would be the easiest thing he would ever do.

The man slunk inside and slid the door closed behind him. For the first time in hours, Edgar walked, stalking his prey. He moved to the door the man had entered and locked it from the outside. There was a back entrance to the hovel Edgar had invited the man to. Or rather, Angela Spark, the online profile that Edgar had created, invited him. Edgar parted the false wall and slipped inside, shutting out the colors of the city until the room was black. He stood silent, seeing only a faint orange glow coming from a lamp in the adjacent room.

"Hello?" The man's timid voice echoed throughout the room ahead of him. "Angela? Are you here?"

"I am," Edgar responded in a malevolently dry tone. He could hear the man scramble to open the door behind him, only to find it sealed. "Raven, is it? That's what your profile says." Edgar turned the corner to see the man with his back against the door. "Which is strange, because your name is Thomas Gillbury. I know where you work, where you live, where your children go to school – off-planet, of course."

Thomas pulled a handgun out of his jacket, only to have it snap instantly from his hand to the floor, as though drawn by a powerful magnet. "What do you want? I have money," the man said, shaking.

"I know you do."

"What's your price?"

Edgar put his hand in front of himself and pulled it downward swiftly. Ten feet away, Thomas's lower jaw ripped away from his skull and clashed against the ground with violent speed.

"My price is that you simply look at this picture." Edgar said calmly through the screams. He drew a tablet from his pocket and turned it to face Thomas. Thomas stumbled backward as Edgar shifted forward, slipping on the blood pouring from his face. The image shown was just a beautiful young woman. Thomas looked at it and screamed louder. "While you die."

Edgar raised his arms and dropped them. Thomas crumpled to the ground under an invisible weight. He began to contort, his body pressing flatter as though ten-thousand pounds were placed upon his back. His screams turned to gurgles. His limbs split open and turned to paste. His eyes popped from his head. Edgar stood there, open palms facing the floor. Edgar stood there, watching.

HAILEY SVARTHOLD

Curiosity is only the first step, love. Treat it like an injured bird; nurse it, care for it and, one day, it will fly. Hailey remembered her father telling her this when she was in school. She found it easier to get lost in thought than before; her memories played like a movie in her head. Her focus was snapped back to the interior of the Progress once they approached Eclipse.

"They're telling us to land on the lower levels." David turned the pilot's chair of the Progress around and waited for a response from the rest of the crew. Hailey only noticed a stoic look coming from Hopper. If he were broadcasting any thoughts, it wasn't on her frequency.

"Are they saying why?" Clara seemed perturbed. "The lower levels are shit."

"I think it has something to do with a government entity on site, but I'm not one hundred percent sure."

"Do you think it's the paladins?"

"I mean, they are trying to hunt me down," Hailey chimed in from the cockpit wall she'd been leaning against, "and Argon is the most likely place for us to get treb clearance out of the sector."

"As far as they're concerned, they think Henry's research died with him and the Magistrate," Clara said. "He staged it to look like a feud between houses. Made it seem like he only revived one person with the sole connection that they both hated Alan Harbrand. Once both of them were gone, all investigation towards his research should end. That was his plan; nobody knows you exist." A brief silence stole the room before Clara could cut through. "Even then, it's difficult to ascertain why they might be on Argon. Do you think their injuries could have been that bad? Bad enough to seek medical attention on this piss-pot?"

"No idea," David dismissed the question and turned his chair back around. "I'll just respond and put us down in the lower levels. I need to do some maintenance, anyways. The sand on B-115 really screwed some of our temporal sensors. I won't be far from the ship."

A few moments later, they were burrowing swiftly into the bowels of Eclipse.

Hailey couldn't fathom what her next steps would be. The best she could come up with was to tour Argon. She was familiar enough, though she had never been, and her body was technically illegal, but nobody really cared. These androids were used for labor and minor tasks throughout some of the more lawless systems. The only reason they were illegal was because of their machine learning software that made the servant more effective in its job over time. Most saw this as harmless, but Emperor Desmond VI did not, instead seeing a slippery slope to an eventual return of AI. After 170 years of unregulated use, these claims had been shown to hold no water.

The Progress slowed and hovered.

"Putting us down on Platform 13," David announced.

"Platform? We weren't given a harbor?" Clara asked.

"Not on short notice like this. Especially because we're trying to keep a low profile. Not a good idea to announce that you're of house Brightwater; too much attention." David looked to Clara and noticed she was deep in thought. "Look, I said I'll be by the ship. If anything goes wrong, I'll call. I'll have Hopper for company, anyways. Right bud?" Hopper lifted his head and stared into David's eyes. David let out a chuckle; Hopper must have projected something funny. "Perfect." He was smiling as he set the ship down.

The side door slid open as Hailey fit her veil back over her head. A miasma of sights and sounds hit her so hard that her vision started to tesselate, distorting shapes and lights together to fill gaps. Hailey looked away to allow the ocular array to refresh and settle down. She turned back slowly, being careful not to look at everything too quickly.

Colors shouldered through the mist and rain, casting rays against every surface. Though constantly alight, every hour in Eclipse was dark in terms of sunlight. Its ramshackle towers and walkways blocked out Barcelona, giving meaning to the city's name. The upper levels were the only ones that got any sunlight, but this was still sparse. Eclipse was so large that it affected local weather. Essentially an artificial mountain, the city would catch clouds and wring out their precipitation onto the citizens below. Only occasionally would Barcelona finally pierce through the clouds of the upper levels, casting aside every color but the deep red it shone.

Hailey learned in her schooling at a young age that the only shadows on Argon were the ones created by its people. Several cartels controlled every manner of business and logistics that kept Argon churning. Hailey found this hard to believe. *Why do people stay? Why would a legitimate businessperson think Eclipse is the best place for them to set up shop?* Hailey only learned later in life that a standard imperial education occasionally left out details. The Emperors Desmond weren't always understanding. She thought she may as well learn how this planet works from up close. With all the time in the galaxy, why not?

Hailey felt something strange. It wasn't the motors in her legs starting up as she took her first step off the Progress, it wasn't the sound of non-human music bouncing around the walkabout, it wasn't the tessellation in her vision. All those feelings were strange, to be sure, but there was something deeper. Something she hadn't felt for years, even before her death. *Curiosity,* and with it, the faintest spark of hope. *Nurse it, care for it and, one day, it will fly.*

SIMON CANSBY

It was only a simple feud between ruling class families, Simon told himself as he thought about Henry Svarthold. *Anger causes people to throw everything away at times. When seeking revenge, dig two graves.* Simon loved the idea of it all being that simple.

"I suppose it will work." Harbrand held his left hand in front of him. "This prosthetic is approved by the Order, correct?" he asked the doctor; the average sized woman seemed a child when standing next to him.

"Of course, sir. Only the best for the Order."

"Good. I would hate to be forced to remove it." Harbrand looked from the hand into the doctor's eyes, "Violently." He turned and walked to Simon. "Let us make our departure, Cansby."

The clinic was extremely high-end for the likes of Eclipse. Simon had an inclination that this may be the best medical facility in Eclipse, possibly all of Argon. The only reason Simon could think that they were brought there was to ensure that the paladins had no reason to complain to the emperor of the current goings-on. That, and they wanted something in return.

"Yes, sir, of course." Simon would love nothing more than to return to Harbor and be near his fellow acolytes and other mentors. "Though I am to inform you that we've been summoned to the Council's Court. They were hoping to petition action from the Order." Simon received the request while Alan was down for surgery.

"Did they give any further information as to the nature of the request?"

"No details to their specific needs. Only that they claim right 235." Right 235 was the right to impose action from any imperial governmental body. When claimed, the right forced the government entity to, at the very least, investigate the case and need. Whoever petitioned and claimed 235 understood the law very well, as the case that won the change in law wasn't well covered in the news. This, paired with the fact that the Persistence and its crew had only just arrived in Eclipse, made everything more suspicious.

"Who makes this claim?" Harbrand's eyes narrowed slightly, seemingly corroborating Simon's doubts.

"Howard Thurston, sir." The name made Harbrand wince slightly before returning to his stony expression.

"Fine," he replied, shortly. "If this is a false report, we can file for an injunction against the *Bandit King*." A title as affectionate as the man himself, the Bandit King was the name some of the ruling class families used to refer to Howard Thurston. Howard liked to use the pretentious *Merchant King*, but most saw through this thin veil to see what he was: a brutal crime lord. If not for his legal team, large sums of money spent on political favor, and a tried-and-true method of keeping secrets, the man would have been rotting away on the prison planet, Ward, for decades.

Howard was the current leader of the Thurston Crime Family, believed to have gained his position by incriminating the former leader, his father, in entity trafficking to have him arrested. Once imprisoned, Howard arranged for his assassination; a staged riot that turned real enough in the aftermath. Hundreds were killed, including the leader of the TCF, leaving his son, Howard, free reign over an empire.

"Until we're called upon, sir," Simon recited.

"Until we're called upon," Alan responded with a nod. "Let's make our way... *upstairs.*"

———

The two paladins made the Climb, a colloquial name for the only walkabout that made it all the way to the higher levels, shifting serpentine through buildings and over alleyways, becoming progressively more wet as they trekked. Fog had settled around them once high enough, though Simon made the realisation that this wasn't a regular fog; these were the clouds.

The day they made the Climb was one of the few that the system's star, Barcelona, was able to present itself from behind the veil surrounding Eclipse. Simon only noticed when the fog they were cutting through started to glow a deep, brick-red, only getting more vibrant as they ascended.

The fog parted like smoke in the wind, revealing they had reached their destination: the Summit. The highest district of Eclipse was of a stark difference to the ones below. Most notable to Simon, was the vegetation. The walkways and common areas of the Summit had all been lined with beautiful gardens and terrariums displaying a verdant bounty of trees and plants. The stone willows of Theridan were somehow able to live and grow while already petrified. The famed singing lilies of Cyclos, extremely rare and endangered, were capable of mimicking sounds like parrots. These were presented in a sealed terrarium, hidden away from any outside noises.

Simon also noticed a daunting figure standing stone-like in an enclosure facing a clear terrarium wall as they passed; the humanoid life-form loomed above the walkabout, separated by a piece of glass. Eight feet tall, it looked like it was made of fungus and tree bark. Simon thought the entity looked quite formidable. He noticed a plaque in front of the display that read, '*Mycelian, Sentinel.*'

The tall myriad towers that normally stood plain white in the fog of the clouds only seemed more regal in the heat of the red giant. Some were glass, whilst others were made of a hybrid ceramic-plastic which was common on newer construction throughout the galaxy. In the sunlight, the towers were spikes glistening with a bright sheen of blood.

"This is what crime can buy you, Cansby." Harbrand seemed to only look forward as they marched. Simon couldn't help himself; he was looking at everything. Simon had grown up poor on an agricultural world in the Shore, never seeing any towers higher than a windmill until he was old enough to depart on his own. Harbor was the first planet he'd been to outside of his birth-world.

"I suppose I can see why people choose that sort of life, then."

"It has its own costs, apart from the money. Look at the people," Harbrand commanded and Simon obeyed. The people ambling around the walkabout certainly looked the part of a higher social class. They had clothes cleaner than what was possible on the lower levels. Wide collars set upon the shoulders of the men, open back dresses for most of the women. *Do they just dress like this all the time? Like they're permanently going to a social event?* "Do you notice anything about them?" Harbrand asked after Simon had some time to observe.

"I'm not sure. I haven't seen a lot of people like this in my life, sir."

"It may take some time before you start to pick up on the clues. These... *people* have every need in their lives solved and cared for. They only had to trade their soul in return." Harbrand's disdain was worn on his sleeve; he hated these kinds of people. "They're all selfish, vapid, stupid, and worst of all, arrogant. All their comfort bought with the pain of others. I don't know what plans the Greater has in store, but I would hope that it involves getting rid of these kinds."

After a long walk and a short wait, they were received at Thurston Tower. Sleek design and elegant decoration made it easy to forget that this was all paid for in blood. Every item In sight, though spotless, was dirty.

The paladins were led into a large oval court room, with a crescent table opposite the door through which they entered. Lining the walls were tall banners that flew family crests and symbols, eight in total. Behind the center seat was the Thurston family crest; a white phoenix rising from ashes, wings spread against a navy-blue background. Seated in the central chair was Howard Thurston, his legal counselor standing to his left at attention. The way he stood made Simon think he might be former military.

"Good sirs!" Howard Thurston proclaimed as the two approached the center of the room, coming to rest on top of the tile art piece adorning the floor beneath them. Shapes corresponding with the banners behind the seats fanned out before them. The seats in the court were empty with the exception being Mr. Thurston's. "Your presence in the Council's Court humbles us."

"As well it should," Harbrand responded, his voice always having no issue filling any space in which he spoke. "It seems as though you and your... *constituents* could use a little humility. I am—"

"Sir Alan Harbrand, I know," Howard interrupted. "I feel your reputation is known galaxy-wide at this point. What was the other name by which you're known? *Sir Alan Harbinger?* Or am I thinking of *The Towering Priest?* I'm certain there's another. Ah! I remember, *Sir Alan The Hateful.*" Harbrand's right hand tightened around his glaive as its pommel rested against the ground. Howard showed only the slightest hint of his enjoyment. "And let us not forget about the acolyte, Simon Cansby, yet to be knighted. You hail from Hemlock, agri-world in The Shore. Truly a storybook path for our young paladin. Such humble beginnings, now apprenticed to one of the galaxy's most famed, and reviled, warriors."

"*ENOUGH,*" Alan commanded, tumultuously. "If all you've summoned us for are hollow insults, then we will take our leave."

"These claims are not hollow, but you're right, let us get down to business." Howard gave a slight wave with his left hand and his legal counsel reacted. The thin man pulled a tablet from his pocket and tapped the screen. A hologram appeared in front of the paladins, showing horrific images of dead men, mangled and seemingly tortured to death. The pictures made Simon uneasy.

The counselor finally spoke. "These are the images taken by our police force here in Eclipse. You'll notice several victims that have been brutally killed. The culprit is suspected to be a serial killer and has yet to be taken into custody." Simon had always been able to pick out details from a larger scene that would otherwise go unnoticed. There was a detail here that Simon couldn't help but notice.

"This seems like work for your police to continue as it is outside of the paladin's purview." Harbrand began to turn to leave. It wasn't though, and Simon knew it.

"Sir Alan, as you may recall, we claim right 235. Please take another look. The suspect may be someone you know personally." Simon was confident that it was. This looked like the work of the arcane. A specific kind of arcane. Several victims appeared to be *pressed.*

"Hoard is a planet that is quite proud of its universities, is it not?" Howard began to interrogate, "Sir Alan, the evidence is clear: this is a practitioner of the arcane." Simon turned his gaze to the smiling Thurston, afraid of what he already knew he would hear. "And not just any school, but one that came from Hoard. *Gravitation.*"

EDGAR THRAWL

Intercepted. You should be getting the feed now.

Edgar received the text through his synaptic response. He squatted under a stairway entrance to a warehouse on the lower levels. Industrial, utilitarian and ugly; this portion of the city was a ghost town at the end of the day.

Loose chains clinked nearby as they swung lazily in the wind. A broken gutter dumped its contents of collected rain onto the hard ground with a random sequence of slaps. A monstrous red sign advertising robotic implants cast every beam and structure in a dark silhouette.

The stolen text feed began to display across Edgar's cornea.

I've got him outside Warehouse 21. Waiting for you, boss.

On my way.

Edgar looked up at the faded paint on the wall of the warehouse. *W17. I was close*, he thought, *just down the street.* He stood and walked onto the damp street, boots clicking as they splashed through the thin film of accumulated water.

His memory of her appeared intermittently, even as he attempted to remain sharp and perceptive. As he passed dreary edifices, he thought he could see her peeking out at him from behind a corner. He fell into memory.

A blurred image of a home on Hoard, a few miles from the university where he taught. He remembered having a stressful day, and, upon walking through the front door, all of it melted away when he saw her. Beaming that smile, she welcomed him home.

Reality rushed back to him at the sound of distant cries and muffled cracks. *A shakedown.* He lithely stepped behind a corner and looked up at the warehouse wall. *W21. Found you.*

He moved along the wall of Warehouse 21, the sounds of beating and interrogation getting louder. A neon sign shifted colors from green to a startling orange. The air, heavy and oppressive, smelled of rust.

He reached the rear of the building, still shimmying along the wall to the corner. Peeking his head around, he saw them: a victim, two thugs beating the victim, and his target.

"Alright, that's enough," Edgar's target commanded his toughs, and they sulked backward. "This is what happens when I don't get my money." His target stood over the bloodied man, pointing down at him. "You have one more week, then I'm throwing you into a recycler," he said, kneeling down to his victim, "right after I make you watch me throw your daughter in."

Edgar had heard enough and rounded the corner.

"Boss." One of the thugs noticed him approaching and pulled a gun. Edgar lifted both arms and dropped them, the two thugs doubled over like they had slipped forward, and their heads cracked sickeningly against the hard ground.

The target pulled a handgun out of his coat and fired, the deafening pop cutting through the constant noise of rain. Edgar responded, pointing his palms at the ground. The man fell, hitting the ground like he had been dropped off the roof of the warehouse they were standing next to.

Edgar mentally took stock of his own body, checking for any sudden pain and was relieved when he found he was uninjured. *He missed,* he thought. "Lucky me, Mr. Langstrom," Edgar said as he walked toward the man bound to the ground. He looked to the victim as he shuffled to his feet. Blood hung from his nose and painted the lower half of his face; the upper half was painted in fear. "Lucky you, too," Edgar said to the man. "Go." The victim turned and ran. Ducking behind Warehouse 22, Edgar heard his footsteps click into the night.

Langstrom remained on the wet ground. He struggled against the gravity well against his back, his gasping only interspersed with muffled whimpering. Edgar thought he looked like a sea creature pulled into open air; eyes widening in fear as clawing breaths brought no reprieve to suffocation. Edgar listened for a moment, letting the tapping of the rain set a backdrop to the music he'd created with the drum of Langstrom's chest cavity. He opened his mouth to begin his prepared statement; Edgar wanted every victim to know why they were dying, but this felt different. He closed his mouth, choosing instead to let the moment be punctuated by labored breaths and subdued whines. He chose instead to let his victim's legacy die in silence; the fire of survival instinct snuffed before it could rage.

Edgar heard the staccato exhales of collapsing lungs as Langstrom stopped twitching. *Better make sure,* he thought before he drew his hand down further. The man's body concaved slowly; an unseen strength pressed its hands against the corpse. He was given audible confirmation as Langstrom's spine snapped with a wet crack. *That should do it.*

Edgar's synapse response triggered, the message scrolled across his cornea.

You should see this

A series of pictures displayed a sleek and regal ship landing on a bay in Eclipse. Two men barrelled out, the larger limping against the smaller. The texts displayed as he verified the images showing the larger of the two striking down a transit command rep.

These are paladins.

They're here.

HAILEY SVARTHOLD

"Wow," Clara remarked. "I've never held a sword." Standing at a walkabout-side kiosk, she lifted a poorly crafted piece of metal.

The human owner of the shop looked at the two of them with a jagged smile then began his rehearsed sales pitch, "This piece was recovered during an archaeological dig on the planet Haldover. Long ago, the denizens of that society were spread far and wide across the galaxy." Clara made a *whooshing* noise as she swung the sword. "They respected skill with blade and were very formidable warriors." Hailey motioned to Clara that she wanted to hold the sword. Clara clumsily handed it over, only slightly winded. Hailey noticed the child-like glee that sparkled in her eyes. She thought it was good to see her smile after B-115. "The Haldovans," the salesman continued, "were wiped out by a plague eons ago. Only remnants, under strict looting laws, are what remains."

Hailey lifted the sword and inspected it. Made of black metal, it dimly reflected the colorful lights nearby. The blade, sharp on one side, bent backward at a drastic angle giving it a particularly alien look. It felt like it was going to fall apart in her hand; the cross guard rattled as she timidly waved it around. Upon lifting the cross guard, she noticed a stamp in the metal that read *Made on Alrinde*. Amused, Hailey handed the sword back to the man at the kiosk. Alrinde was a planet in the Inner Arm where numerous products are cheaply manufactured.

"You got a good deal on this one," she remarked. "It's a one-of-a-kind artifact."

"Yes, and I pass the savings on to you!"

"I'm sure you do."

His smirk dwindled as Hailey gently corralled Clara, moving her away from the conman.

Clara looked over her shoulder as they departed. "He has throwing stars, though," she informed Hailey with a disappointed tone.

From their brief time getting to know one another, Hailey saw that Clara was extremely intelligent. She was diligent, but caring. The occasional smile broke through when David or Hopper said something funny, but the summary of her character was sheer focus. As a scientist and a friend, Hailey noticed that Clara rarely swayed from the task or goal at which she was aimed.

To see her now, alight at the sight of a sharp piece of metal, only grew Hailey's affection for her. The roles had reversed for a moment; Clara took care of Hailey as she rose from the dead, and now Hailey was guiding Clara away from a scam. *Is this what having a sister feels like?* The thought took her by surprise, and Hailey released her hold on Clara.

They approached another kiosk positioned in the middle of the walkabout. Bar stools surrounded three sides of the structure. Lit with a stark white light, two men cooked and served food to patrons sitting at the stools.

Clara's head lifted as she caught the scent. "Hey, do you—" she started and looked at Hailey. The words caught in her throat as she was reminded what Hailey was.

"It's fine," Hailey said in a reassuring tone.

Clara sighed deeply, "Thank you. I'm so hungry."

They sat, and Clara shyly signaled for *one, please.* A Larscian lumbered by on four legs, grunting deeply. A human man walked abreast with it, speaking as though they were catching up on recent events. The Larscian wore what looked like a handmade blanket over its back covering its deep red pelt. Hailey stared; she had seen non-humans before but not this close, and not this many.

A plate of sizzling meat and vegetables was placed in front of Clara and her eyes widened. She dug in with chop sticks, groaning after the first bite. Hailey looked back to her and tried to think of something to say. *I barely know this woman, yet she let everything go in order to uphold an oath older than both of us.*

"So..." Hailey began, searching for anything to ask Clara, anything to fill the silence. Clara lifted her head with a guilty look, like she was too distracted by food to remember that she wasn't alone. "...Siblings?" *You know she has siblings, dipshit,* Hailey scolded herself.

"Broffers," she informed her through the food in her mouth. She swallowed and clarified, "Brothers, three of 'em." She seemed to drop into a pensive haze then, for just a moment. Hailey thought it was likely that scenes of her childhood were flashing in front of her eyes. Clara snapped from it almost as soon as she had fallen into it. "You?" she asked as she took another bite.

"No. Only child." Hailey wished she had siblings. Maybe if she had an older brother, she wouldn't have needed to worry about the role of leadership. Maybe if she had a sister, she wouldn't have felt so alone after her mother had left.

They fell into a silence broken only by the rapid goings-on nearby. The sizzles and clanks of pans, the chatter of a hundred different languages, the constant taps of raindrops against the walkabout.

Only half-finished, Clara pushed the plate away from her and turned her body to Hailey. "Can I ask you something? Something that might be a little too personal?" The focus that Hailey was used to had returned to Clara's eyes.

"I suppose," Hailey answered after a moment's consideration.

Clara stared at her briefly. "Why did you do it?"

"Ok, that's—"

Clara reached out and set her hand on Hailey's. "I'm only trying to understand you, Hailey. I'm not asking because I think you didn't have a reason. It's just that when people make the decision you did, you normally can't talk to them about it after the fact."

The hand and warm tone began to dissolve the barriers Hailey had put up, and she found herself staring blankly; a reflection of what was happening in her mind. She hadn't thought about it since it happened and now she was trying to dredge her memory, looking for any remnant of her justification for the most important decision she had ever made.

"I..." she started. "Loneliness. I think. No siblings, of course. My mother left when I was young, and I haven't spoken to her since. I don't know if she's alive. My father gave me some reasons as to why she disappeared, but I never got to hear it from her. After that, I fell in love. I was still young and naïve; he wasn't going to stay and be mine, he couldn't. The loneliness and desperation turned to anger. Any time I looked at Henry, I thought about how he had driven my mother away. I didn't know if that was true, but I made myself believe it.

"Then there was *legacy* and *duty.* I wasn't given a choice and the rage grew and festered any time I was reminded I was nobility." Hailey felt like if ever she was going to cry, it was then. Her heart ached, and she didn't know how that was possible. Clara's apathetic gaze remained fixed on Hailey. She felt like Clara was welcoming every piece of information and turning it over in her head, not missing a single detail. "I don't know if what I did was smart," Hailey continued, "I don't even know if that decision was right or justified. I just know that it was mine." *It was my decision,* she reminded herself. *It was my decision.*

Catharsis released the levies holding back anxiety and tension, and Hailey could feel her shoulders relax. Even in an artificial body, the subconscious tendency to stay tense had to be overcome manually.

Clara smiled softly, warmly at Hailey. "Thank you for telling me." Hailey only nodded. They lifted themselves from the stool seating to enter the throng of people surrounding them.

"Where next?" Hailey asked, voice shaking slightly.

Clara shook her head and sighed, "We can get treb clearance later. You pick." She smiled again at Hailey, motioning to her to lead the way.

Is this what having a sister feels like?

SIMON CANSBY

"Don't stare," Harbrand commanded quietly. Simon hadn't noticed he was staring, mouth agape, at the lumbering entity as it strolled past. On four legs, its slow footsteps planted to the walkabout with a dull thud. A human man walked alongside the creature, seemingly having a conversation with it. "A Larscian," he informed Simon as they stood outside on a lower-level walkabout, every nearby eye falling upon them; Simon sensed the irony as he was receiving the same stare he was just giving to the large non-human. "I haven't seen one in some time. A little... intimidating up close."

A handmade blanket draped over the back of the Larscian above red fur. It grunted as it passed; Simon couldn't tell if it was looking at him, but he felt like his abashment was easily observable, regardless.

"Lock's clear," an associate of Howard Thurston's announced; she had been called to help them with security at some of the crime scenes. The door slid open to the hovel.

"Wait out here," Harbrand ordered in a low growl to the security associate. "We'll let you know if you're needed further. Cansby, with me."

The two paladins stepped past the threshold and into a dark apartment. The smell took Simon first; iron-rich blood mixing with old sweat and decay. The stench of blood only seemed to be a fresh layer over the aged, unwashed filth that was persistent before.

Simon reached up the wall and flicked on the light switch.

"Greater save us," Harbrand muttered under his breath.

Glossy eyes stared at them from the floor. The man lay flat on his chest, with his head looking left to the door. His left arm pointed outward; his right lay parallel with the body. An indentation formed in the flooring under his body. A small metal object protruded from his temple.

Simon walked slowly around the corpse and reviewed what he saw, despite his heart screaming at him to run. Simon knelt and moved his right arm slightly. With the bones fragmented and the skin bright purple, he guessed that it had been flattened. The effect seemed to stop just below the shoulder. He shifted his attention to the object in the man's temple. A trinket the size of Simon's thumb, stuck halfway out of his skull.

The apartment was filthy. It didn't look, to Simon's best guess, that it had been ransacked, but that this victim lived in squalor. The recent struggle seemed to be isolated to the area nearest the body, suggesting that he'd caught the victim off-guard.

"Why him?" Simon wondered aloud.

"That's the problem with serial killers," Harbrand said as he stared at the corpse in disgust. Simon wasn't sure if the disgust was aimed at what had happened or at the victim himself. It could have been both. "Justification is internal, and always flawed. What is irrefutable to them seems like mania to the rest of us. We might not know what this person was thinking until well after the fact."

Simon thought on that, allowing the words to tumble in his head as he continued to examine the corpse. He knelt next to the victim's left arm. "This arm's uninjured," Simon stated.

"And?"

He looked the body up and down and a theory popped into his head. "What if the perpetrator was trying to get information from the victim?" Harbrand responded with a hesitantly curious look. "The floor is slightly concave where the body lays, and the right arm has been flattened completely, but the left arm was left to move freely."

"How would that help get information from the victim?"

"They could have needed the victim to point at something for them. A map, a picture? Something on a tablet, maybe? I would bet that the trinket in the skull was the kill shot. Succinct and quiet, it got the job done when all the information was gathered."

"So, let's say you're right, then this person is going around killing people for what?" Harbrand speculated. "What do you think they're after? Drug or weapon deal that went wrong? Somebody owes them money?"

"Honestly, I'm not sure. It seems unlikely that someone came all the way from Hoard to commit crimes for something as small as drug money. We'll need to see more crime scenes to get a better understanding," Simon admitted.

"Yes, but I like where your head's at," Harbrand said, "This will give us a different angle to view the case... and I'm sure we'll have another corpse to look at soon enough."

As though on cue, their tablets notified them of another crime scene in need of investigation. They read the details and Harbrand sighed.

Harbrand instructed the security associate to gather evidence as they began to depart. *Regardless of their motivation*, Simon thought as he looked back to the corpse on the floor, *they're angry.* Glossy eyes met with his for a moment longer before he turned and left.

EDGAR THRAWL

"Please," the young man was crying, tears mixing with blood as they settled on the cut on his face. "I don't know what else to tell you. The paladins showed up and the tall one hit me."

"WHY ARE THEY HERE?" Edgar yelled.

"They- they needed medical attention. I swear. I asked why they couldn't have taken care of this on their ship and the tall one hit me."

"Why did they go to the Summit? WHO SUMMONED THEM?"

"Please," the young man was sobbing, words becoming unintelligible as he sat on the floor, hands bound above his head and tied to a pipe protruding from the wall. "Please, I went home after, I swear, I don't know why they were asked to go the Summit."

One of the young man's legs was mangled and laid out before him on the floor. Edgar held his hand out before him and tightened his grip around nothing. The young man began to scream, and Edgar shoved a cloth into his mouth, his leg writhing on its own. After a few moments, Edgar ceased the torture and ripped the cloth from the young man's mouth.

"Timmett, I'm disappointed," Edgar explained as Timmett continued to sob. "Had you have given me something to work with, I might not have even brought this up."

"Please, I—"

"Quiet. You're a host, correct?" Timmett gave a timid nod. "So, you're aware of what goes on in the back rooms of Evelesce for high-end clients. You know what they pay for."

"I do, I'll tell you anything you want to know about it." Timmett hurried out the words, a glimmer of hope starting to show in his voice.

"I'm sure you'll do anything to save your skin. No, I have all the information I need on that. I only ask because you hosted these events with no regard for anyone that may have suffered. Are you not guilty of these crimes yourself?"

"I never—"

"Why am I asking, I already know what you'll say." He shoved the cloth back into Timmett's mouth. Edgar pulled his empty hand down violently. A short, muffled scream was silenced when Timmett was crushed suddenly, folded in half where he sat.

HAILEY SVARTHOLD

"Thine life, I shall take with mine own blade!" the cloaked man yelled to his aggressor.

"Thou may try, my brother. But heed my words: our familiarity with one another shalt not save thee. For once we may have toiled side by side, this can be no longer. Come with me, and answer for thine crimes." *It's been almost 2400 years,* Hailey thought while watching the men argue, *are we ever going to let go of pretentious Shakespearean dialogue?*

"Thou'st call me brother, but see not what I have done, and the good I have created thus. Trust me as you once did."

"Such a cost cannot be forgiven. There may be merit to using evil to create good, but a line has been drawn."

"What Shakespeare piece is this?" Hailey leaned in and asked Clara.

Clara widened her grin to make a grimace and whispered. "I think it's an original."

"Oh, so that's why it's so bad." This was only corroborated by the fact that there were only four people in attendance at the streetside performance apart from Hailey and Clara.

"I give in, but know this," the first man continued, "I shall never feel remorse. No matter the punishment." He fell to his knees, bowed his head and raised his hands, showing he was ready to be put under arrest.

The lights dimmed as the play came to an end out of nowhere. Confusion settled amongst the 'crowd' as they started to applaud sparsely. *Was that the conclusion? Who wrote this?* The cast returned to the stage to give their final bow. Among the two men was a woman from an earlier scene that still had her shirt torn open. It appears whoever wrote this play wanted to shoe-horn in some nudity, as Hailey couldn't think of any other reason why that character even graced the stage; her tits were introduced almost as soon as she was.

"Well, we won't be getting that time back," Clara said with a snide tone. A reactionary giggle broke free from Hailey. *I didn't know I could do that,* she thought. *Laugh.* She felt it first in her chest, which must have been her mind filling in the missing data, like how tinnitus is just the mind filling in missing hearing. "We can get treb clearance down the road, then after we can get our fortunes read." Hailey thought this sounded fun. *Fun.*

They departed, wandering through the lower-level walkabout, passing beggars, non-humans, weirdos, musicians, and drug addicts. With kiosks and bodegas littered throughout, the two were offered all manner of strange sundries. Three different shopkeepers each offered aphrodisiacs, another was a purveyor of secrets, another claimed to be bringing goods from outside of the galaxy. All of this painted by the miasma of colorful lights that hung everywhere. Hailey was enthralled. This was such a stark difference from the clean markets of Nymeria, the capital city of Arcturus.

Hailey turned to look at someone shouting about a discount, only to find herself within arm's length of a reflection; a full-array humanoid drone. The same type she inhabited stood, still and lifeless, in front of her. Hailey took a step toward it, but the android was recalled by its owner with a simple command. Watching it leave in silence, she heard Clara call out to her. Beckoned by a simple command, Hailey followed.

Purpose, Hailey thought, wandering in a haze. *I need to find mine. I have nothing and everything to worry about. I don't need to eat, I don't need to sleep. I can't fall back on vices and base desires. When everything that biological beings need to balance is taken out of the equation, what's left? What even is purpose? Some find theirs by seeking a profession that can pay for things that make them happy. Others seek it in family. I have none of that. I need to find purpose. Or make it for myself.*

"Here. This kind of place will handle most things involving the more boring parts of government." Clara stopped in front of a shop that the proprietors of which had done their very best to make look official. A faded white façade had been painted over in several spots to cover graffiti; above the door hung a bright sign that read, '*Post*'. They stepped inside.

A gentle bell tone sounded from a hidden speaker as they opened the door. The interior was a stark difference to the surrounding buildings. White strip lights lit the retail floor which was decorated with clean rows of shelves housing a variety of envelopes and shipping boxes, some sophisticated and vacuum sealed, others made of recycled paper composite.

Hailey took stock of her tepid surroundings. "I didn't think we still used the post anymore. We have the QI network, shouldn't that have made all of this obsolete?"

"You'd think, but a lot of government documents still have to be physically sent," Clara responded, touching an envelope as they passed, "and people still need packages delivered," she shrugged slightly.

The two approached the unmanned front desk. On the counter in front of them was a button, above which, taped to the counter, a small handwritten sign read, '*Ring Bell for Service*'. Clara reached out and touched the button gently. In one of the rooms behind the counter, a sharp buzzer sounded. In the same moment, the two could hear clamoring and metal hitting the ground, along with a brisk "FUCK" yelled in frustration.

After a few more moments of listening to someone shuffling through the mess, a Cyclan popped his head around the corner and looked at the two. Tall and thin, Cyclans had grey skin, large heads and all-black, almond shaped eyes. Historically, they'd felt animosity towards humans since the time of the Conquest. They were the first species to make contact with the human race before they started reaching out to the stars, and that contact wasn't always forthcoming or gentle.

"Yes, what?" he asked the two sharply.

"Hi, we need treb clearance, can you do that here?" Clara responded in a friendly voice. The Cyclan stepped out in a huff, clearly frustrated. Hailey heard the door tone sound behind her, another customer entered, but she didn't care to look.

"Yes, fine," the Cyclan said as he began to type on the glass screen in front of him. "Ship ID, and business."

"Here's the ID." Clara pulled out her tablet and quickly sent the info. "Regarding business, we are a shipping vessel heading back to the Galactic Commons."

The Cyclan stood and silently tapped on the screen for a few moments. Without looking up, he stated flatly, "Denied."

"...What?" Clara was starting to look nervous. "What do you mean '*Denied*'?"

"Your ship ID is out of date. I can update it, but processing will take... 43 days, RGT."

"*Are you kidding me?*"

"No, I don't do that."

"Hey, can they use mine?" a gruff voice sounded off behind them. "I'm a government contractor, I know mine is good to go." The man stepped forward and sent his information to the Cyclan. He was built sturdy, with a short mutton chop beard and an old white hat that read, '*California Republic*'.

The Cyclan took another moment tapping the display. "Yes, this will work. But their vehicle is now on a sub-registry with yours. Any criminal activity will be tied to yours until their ID is updated."

"That'll be fine." The man turned and gave a sympathetic smile to Clara. "Once these two get back to the Commons, they'll update their info, I'm sure."

"Very well." A few more taps at the screen. "Both ships are set for transit out of Trebuchet Hastings. Can I help with anything else?"

"No, that'll do." The three began walking out of the shop.

"Thank you so much for helping us. I'm Clara." Clara held out her hand, Bill grabbed and shook it.

"Bill." Displaying the same smile as before. Bill released her hand. "I've never been a fan of bureaucracy. That was just gonna waste everyone's time. I trust you'll renew your ship's ID once you're back in the Commons?"

Clara gave an enthusiastic nod. "Of course. Thank you."

"No problem, just try to fly under the speed limit."

"Are you parked nearby?"

"No. I'm up on mid-level. I needed treb clearance, but I heard there was a place that makes the best ramen down here. Had to give it a shot." The group exited the store and stood in the rain. "I best be on my way back, but you two should be careful. The lower levels can get pretty mean."

"Of course, thank you again."

Bill gave a nod and a slight wave and walked away, disappearing into the crowd after a few moments.

"That was very lucky," Hailey finally spoke up.

"Extremely. We were almost stranded." The two left, seeking fortune tellers before heading to the ship.

———

After passing assorted peoples and sights along the walkabout, Clara and Hailey came upon a soothsayer seated cross-legged on a rug, a small canopy hung just above her head to keep her out of the rain. The old woman had thin lines tattooed on her face, and several teeth replaced with different colored gemstones. Next to her was a sign that read, '*Dreamwalker*'.

"That's surprising," Clara remarked, "I didn't expect a Dreamwalker to be all the way out here. They're usually hanging out in the Shore with all the other practitioners of foresight."

"What did you expect when you said we'd get our fortunes told?" Hailey wasn't very familiar with any kind of practice in prophecy or foresight.

"I have no idea," Clara shrugged. "Tarot cards?"

The two walked over to the old woman. She tilted up her head as they approached to reveal two milk-white eyes. "I have walked among many lives," she told the two. "Come to me, I will tell you where I've been." She held out a frail hand.

Clara went first. The old woman held her hand and thought for a moment, then said in a worn voice, "The loyalist. Strange, considering the choices you've made, and will continue to make. You are, in your heart, a good person after all. Loyal in a... unique sort of way. But will they be worth it? The choices you've made?" Clara pulled her hand away sharply but didn't say anything, the smile wiped from her face. Hailey watched her and noticed she was deep in thought.

"Are you ok?" she whispered to Clara from behind her veil.

Without looking away from her hand, Clara gave a nod from behind pursed lips.

"Do I go now? Will this even work on me?"

"I... I'm not sure."

"Fair enough." Hailey planted her hand firmly into the old woman's.

"Oh, darling. Your hands are so cold." She gave Hailey a half smile. "I'm only getting one word. This is strange, because I normally get a range of thoughts and emotions tied to the person and their experiences." The old woman continued to hold Hailey's hand, silently processing.

After a few moments, Hailey asked nervously, "What's the word?"

"Oathbreaker."

SIMON CANSBY

Fear, anticipation, regret, guilt. The first two made sense; the Carthian was in a stressful situation. Regret could be explained away as well. Maybe he failed to do something that could've helped. But guilt? Why guilt? Especially when paired with the other emotions, it seemed as though maybe the Carthian wasn't a victim. What was he doing there?

"Cansby." Simon stirred when he heard his name from the other side of the room. "Come here and get this." Harbrand pointed to a piece of the victim's clothing on the ground; a boot, with the foot still in it. Simon hurried to do as he was told and picked up the boot. "What does it say?"

Simon read the label aloud, "Property of Halsin Corp. It has a name written in ink underneath: Timmett Wilson."

"That's the fifth victim tied to the cartels here in Eclipse. This seems more like a vendetta than the work of a serial killer. There's something Thurston isn't telling us." They stood over the remains of Timmett, unrecognizable in its current state. Bones jutting up from the cadaver, blood pooling in large quantities underneath, and limbs folded grotesquely under immense pressure made it clear that no one could have displayed this kind of force without the help of arcane practices.

Harbrand called Howard Thurston via his tablet. Simon remembered the young man on the floor. It had only been a few days prior when Harbrand struck him down and Simon helped him back to his feet.

"Sir Alan, what can I do for you?" Howard picked up, sounding almost cheerful.

"You're hiding information about these victims, Thurston."

"I believe you'll need to speak to my lawyers about that."

"Cut the shit. We've examined five crime scenes and the only things that tie the victims together are the method by which they're killed and their employers. All of them had been employed by you or your... associate's cartels."

"I prefer the term, '*corporation*'."

"I don't care. We're missing some valuable information that could help us find the suspect. This clearly isn't the work of a serial killer like you specified, this looks more like a vigilante."

Some silence followed for a short time before Howard responded, "I... I need to get back to you, paladin." The call ended.

Simon broke the silence after the call, "Sir, there's something you should know about this victim." Harbrand turned his gaze to Simon silently. "We've met this one already."

"When?"

"Well, sir, he's the young man that you struck when we got off the Persistence. I helped him up and he told me his name: Timmett." Simon showed the boot to him.

"So, this victim died after we arrived in Eclipse. The killer knows we're here."

It seems like everyone does. Simon noticed the gears turning behind Harbrand's eyes. He was coming up with a plan.

In the moments after they left the house, Simon had time to think. In the steady rain illuminated by a nearby purple sign, he thought about Henry Svarthold. Harbrand had spoken poorly of him in the past, but Simon knew there was bad blood between the two families.

He had learned in his time at the Evening Library on Harbor that the Svartholds had helped the neighboring Sector's Bannerlord, Karakura, during a territory skirmish decades ago, before Henry was named lord of the Outer Reach. Gunnar Svarthold deployed his fleet to assist in a dogfight above Orchard, an agricultural world near the boundary of the Inner Reach and the Core. The Karakura fleets were still recovering from a non-human rebellion and stretched too thin to win the battle for the system.

The Harbrands had previously tried to claim the territory in the name of the Core and saw this as an opportunity to strike. They weren't expecting Svarthold participation and suffered a staggering defeat.

Simon had silently questioned Harbrand's integrity involving matters of state and conflicts of interest, though doing so aloud could mean treason. Still, he felt something stir when Howard Thurston mentioned Harbrand's past. *One of the galaxy's most famed, and reviled, warriors.* How much was true? And did Henry really give up *everything* to destroy Harbrand when his family had already won decades ago?

After a short walk in silence, they had found their way back to the Persistence. Bill was listening to an eclectic mix of non-human music over the sound system; soft strings plucking an arpeggiated pattern over a brassy bassline.

"Turn that off," Harbrand commanded as they entered the flight deck of the ship, just behind Bill's chair.

"Aye." Bill reached down and cut the music short. "I found some vendors selling cool stuff while I was out wanderin'. Like this music." He ignored Bill.

"Simon, I think I have an idea." Harbrand leaned his glaive in the corner and turned to Simon with a flash of a sinister smile.

HAILEY SVARTHOLD

Oathbreaker. Hailey sat aboard the Progress adrift from herself, ruminating on that word. *Oathbreaker.* Henry had broken every oath he had ever taken when he continued his research. *Oathbreaker.* The lord and sworn protector of the Outer Reach, forsaking his duty to the empire to save his research and his daughter.

Is this all that I am? An artifact of one man's hubris? I have nothing but the endless pursuit of finding my own purpose, watching everything age around me while I linger.

The crew of the Progress wandered around Hailey prepping for flight while she sat on a flight bench, except for Hopper, who stood staring with his shining obsidian eyes, dying to know how Hailey was feeling. Hailey didn't notice.

"We are good to go, looks like," David announced from his flight chair, snapping Hailey away from her thoughts. She looked up to notice Hopper turning his head to look at David. "I feel you there, bud," David responded to Hopper's silent communication as he craned his head to look at him. "Just a couple of days in superluminal and we'll be in the Commons."

Hailey thought about Bill and how lucky they'd been. *Hopefully nothing happens to the Progress that'll get him in any trouble; this ship is carrying one of the most wanted entities in the galaxy, if I'm to ever be discovered.*

The Progress had lifted from its pad and broke through Argon's atmosphere. "You ready?" Hailey didn't notice Clara approach.

"Just gotta take a quick shit," Hailey responded as she looked up to Clara. She cracked a little smile at the joke. Hailey tried to smile back.

"Good to know," Clara said as she sat next to Hailey. "We think going to Titan will be the best next step."

"*Titan?*" Hailey whipped her head to look at Clara. "Are you *insane?*"

"Look, I know it's daunting, but as long as you lie low, we should be just fine. No one knows you exist after all."

"Let's just hope I don't bump into the emperor."

"You know that's ridiculous. He rarely leaves his palace, let alone goes outside of the city. No one's seen him outside of court since three emperors ago."

Hailey knew the emperor was a mystery to most, and the emperor's throneworld was almost as eccentric. Titan was the seat of the empire. The artificial planet had more hiding places than the settled planets had moons. Titan had started as a space station; the primary forward base, shipyard and command post during the conquest of the galaxy. Over time, the station had had pieces added for expansion. Almost a thousand years later, it had grown to the size of a planet. The hiding places were due to the haphazard methods of construction: stairwells leading to nowhere, holes dropping for miles, and hotspots of intermittent irregular gravity were a few of the anomalies.

The strangeness of the planet did not mean that it was lacking in resplendence. Some of the most prestigious universities were on Titan, as well as recently established arcane institutions. The Galactic Commons was the hub of trade throughout the galaxy, with Titan right in the center.

Hailey felt uneasy about it, but she knew she could hide amongst the chaos of the emperor's throneworld, as long as she was careful.

"Fine," she gave in to Clara, "I'll try to stay out of everyone's—"

-Rebooting

Hailey saw the word flash in front of her in blackness, followed by her ocular array turning back on. She looked around as her vision cleared, noticing she was lying on the floor. Her binaural microphone turned on moments later.

"What just happened?"

"I'm having David run some scans." Hailey recognized Clara's voice, she and Hopper leaning over her.

"Did I pass out?"

"I don't know if I would call it that. Did you see any text outputs?"

"All it said was rebooting."

"You just did a hard reboot?" David asked, just out of sight.

"I have no idea."

"What does that mean?" Clara asked David, still kneeling next to Hailey.

David was silent until he walked in from the cockpit. He looked at the group and, after a breath, said, "It means the engram is decaying faster than we thought it would."

EDGAR THRAWL

I threw away my entire life. I didn't have a purpose once she was gone. I want to burn it down. I'm not finished. I don't want to hurt the paladins, but I have to finish my work. I can't let them get away with everything they've done. Edgar sat alone in a lower-level bar replete with cheap liquor and even cheaper company, as far as the upper-level citizens were concerned. *A hell of our own design lies just under their noses, and they couldn't care less.* Edgar felt all the more justified. *If no one else will tear this place down, then I will.*

Edgar received a notification. He stood and swiped on his tablet, sending credits to the bartender. Downing the rest of his drink, Edgar walked out into the damp of the walkabout. Though he hated it, Edgar had gotten used to the smell. Damp and mold, piss and decay, chemicals and exhaust fumes. His tablet received a new message.

On the move.

Edgar affixed his hood on his head and began to walk.

The younger one's on his own. It looks like he's just wearing normal clothes, no armor.

Edgar read the messages being fed to his tablet, with a corresponding picture of the young paladin.

Lower level, southbound on walkabout B.

The paladin melted into the crowd. *It looks like he wants a little bit of 'off the books' fun,* Edgar thought as he watched the young man slink into an alleyway toward a brothel. Edgar followed. *I'm sorry, young one. Hopefully, I can convince you to look the other way.* The paladin looked over his shoulder, but Edgar kept his pace. Through the bustle of the streets and alleyways, he was almost invisible. Edgar made use of his unassuming looks and stature to blend into the common goings-on wherever he went. Once, he hated it. To be looked over by everyone made him feel worthless. Until she found him.

One final look over his shoulder and the young paladin passed beyond the threshold of a questionable establishment. A single illuminated sign read, '*Sleepless*,' in orange above the door. Edgar lingered. He counted to 90 before following to give his target time to settle in. Before the end of his count, his tablet received another message.

Target has landed. Signing off.

Edgar read it, silently thanked his impromptu partner, and counted the last few numbers in his head. *88...89...90.* Edgar entered Sleepless; a narrow, dimly lit hallway flanked by private rooms. On his left, a service counter with a lone proprietor. Edgar lowered his hood and looked at the clerk; a human, stocky and plain, looked back at him.

"Welcome to Sleepless. Please take your pick from one of our private rooms. The kiosk inside will display all our options," the clerk told Edgar.

"Any rooms I should avoid?" Edgar asked, hoping to secretly glean some information as to the paladin's whereabouts.

"Any of the rooms will have access to your choice of any of our services. Room 4 is the only one occupied at the moment."

"Thank you." *Room 4, it is.*

Edgar ambled down the hall, taking his time. He was hoping that by the time he got to his destination, the clerk would be distracted by other duties and fail to notice him.

Room 4 sat at the end of the hallway. Edgar looked back at the clerk, and he was gone. *Now's your chance.* He tapped on the screen outside the room. *Unlocked. The kid's not very experienced.* Edgar's nerves were boiling. Everything seemed to be a haze. *I don't want to do this, but I have to get him off my trail. I don't want to kill him, but I will.* Edgar tapped the '*open*' button on the screen.

The door slid open silently. In front of him was the paladin, sitting in a chair facing away from the door, clearly distracted by the woman dancing just behind the glass opposite him. Neither noticed as Edgar closed the door silently. Using the room's internal touchscreen, he locked the door and deactivated the pane glass. It went from transparent to opaque almost instantly.

The paladin stood and Edgar faced his palms downwards. The force of arcane gravity forced the young man to the floor, on his hands and knees. He grunted and coughed as Edgar knelt close.

"Young one, I do not wish to hurt you, but you and your commander have gotten too close."

"What... what is this?" the young man asked, struggling against his own weight.

"Gravity. I figured you'd be more familiar as your order is made to understand the arcane."

"What do you want?"

"Justice, young one. I never thought that the order would make it all the way out to Argon. The cartels are doing gravely evil things out here. Far worse than the crimes I've committed."

The young paladin winced as he held himself up from the floor. "What crimes?"

"Entity trafficking. They're kidnapping humans and non-humans alike from all over the galaxy, usually in less monitored systems, and bringing them here. They operate with near impunity. Once sold to different parties, select individuals are taken back to Eclipse. Here, they are set upon by upper-class individuals with insatiable urges. Some are tortured, others are raped, some both. Whether out of rage, boredom or sick sexual fantasy, their reasoning makes no difference." Edgar reached down and grabbed the paladin by his face and forced him to look up from the floor and into his eyes. "I'm going to kill every single one of them and burn this place down." Edgar let go of his face and stood. "I'm just sorry that you have been caught in the middle. I wanted you to know that this isn't personal."

"Any time, now," the paladin said quietly.

"What?"

Edgar didn't notice the door open behind him. He almost didn't notice his left arm being severed below the shoulder. Shock, surprise and terror set in as he grabbed where his arm once was. Edgar collapsed to the floor and shuffled in panic to the wall.

"NO, NO, NO, WHAT HAVE YOU DONE?" he screamed, eyes welling with tears. He looked up to see a tower of a human standing in front of him with the glaive that cut his arm off pointed in his face.

"If you try anything, I will not hesitate," the man warned. Edgar looked to see the young one standing up. Edgar's spell had ceased once his arm was removed. Now, the young paladin could move freely.

"By the right bestowed upon us by the Emperors Desmond, I place you under arrest. Your charges are murder, conspiracy to commit murder, and unlawful use of arcane practices," the young paladin stated with authority.

"I CANNOT STOP!" Edgar howled. "THEY TOOK HER FROM ME!" Gathering himself, he looked to the young paladin. "If you have any sense of justice, think of what I've told you." *I may die, but my mission must live on.* "Below Evelesce, that's where they bring the victims. YOU MUST BURN IT D—" Edgar was interrupted by the blunt end of a glaive to the face.

OATHBREAKER

KENJI KARAKURA

"Rear Admiral, we're beginning deceleration. Drift from trebuchet throw is at 3000 K. We'll arrive at Arcturus in approximately 32 hours." From his perch at the center of the command deck, Rear Admiral Kenji Karakura stoically received information from his sailors. With his arms held behind his back, Kenji stood and evaluated the situation. He aimed to show authority in everything he did. His hair was immaculate, cut every other week. His dress blues were pressed, with not a button out of place. His posture was statuesque. Kenji did everything he could so his fear would not betray him.

"3000 K is manageable. Open comms to Admiral Karakura." Hiroshi Karakura was the highest-ranking admiral of the Karakura Navy, the brother of the Lord of the Inner Reach, and Kenji's father.

"Aye, sir. Comms open," the comms officer responded.

"This is Rear Admiral Kenji Karakura of the Maelstrom, fifth fleet," Kenji recited his credentials to the hidden microphone in the command station in front of him; a circular display showing three dimensional readouts of the fleet. "We are beginning deceleration and will arrive in 32 hours. How copy, Horizon?"

"This is Grand Admiral Karakura of the Horizon," the admiral's dry tone rang from the speaker in the command deck. "Our trajectory shows orbit with Arcturus in approximately 27 hours. Fall in line and arrive with the rest of the fleet, Rear Admiral." Anxiety flared in Kenji's heart and sent surges to his arms and legs.

"Yes sir, Grand Admiral. Adjusting course now." Kenji gave a nod to his navigator as a sign of command to follow what the admiral had said. *Everyone here heard what he said.*

The navigator, Takeshi Yamada, after working at his station for a few moments, turned and gave a confirming nod. The readout in front of Kenji changed.

"Grand Admiral, we are now showing a trajectory of 27.7 hours until orbit."

"That will suffice, Rear Admiral." The comms went silent. Kenji stood just as silent, thinking about everything that could go wrong on his first mission as Rear Admiral. Kenji was the youngest admiral in the entire Karakura Navy at only 35 years old, RGT.

"XO Yamada, you have the deck. I'll be in my chambers," Kenji commanded after a long bout of internal dread had passed.

———

Kenji lay awake and thought about the mission and Karakura loyalty. Svarthold succession was in question and there were whispers of a power grab, most likely from old aggressors from the Core, like the Harbrands. Because of their help in the territory skirmishes, the Karakuras held deep devotion to their friends in the Outer Reach. When the ruling council of Arcturus asked for assistance, Chiyo Karakura, the Lord of the Inner Reach, sent the fleet.

After a short and fitful sleep, Kenji stirred and returned to command. At the command table, he ordered everyone at ease and asked for a status report.

"Sir, there are other ships in the system. Their headings are for Arcturus," Yamada informed.

"Do we know to whom they belong?"

"No sir. We've only just caught them on long-range sensors."

Kenji had a feeling of who they might be. "Any word from the fleet?"

"None as of yet, sir. The Horizon has continued its speed and heading."

"Very well. We'll do the same." *An easy-enough command, anyone could've made that choice.*

The unknown fleet, as well as Arcturus, finally came into scope, several hours later. "Sir, we're getting a wide-band broadcast from the Horizon to the fleet," Yamada announced. Before Kenji could say anything, the call played throughout the command deck, accompanied by a projection of Hiroshi Karakura.

"Fifth fleet, this is your Grand Admiral. We have identified the ships on course for Arcturus. It appears they are the Blackhat attack fleet." *The Blackhats? If they're involved, the Lords of the Core shouldn't be far behind.* Kenji felt another wave of dread pull the blood from his fingertips. Hiroshi continued, "We have opened hails to the Blackhat fleet, but with no answer. Additionally, there has been no response from Arcturus, which leads me to believe that their communications have been attacked. Prepare for battle."

"To your stations!" Kenji commanded. "Prepare for battle!" The command room was set ablaze as the lights changed from a warm white to a deep, searing red. Sailors began moving in every direction. Kenji felt like he was going to pass out.

"Sir, we have more ships on scope. In orbit around Arcturus, we only just caught sight as they moved to this side of the planet."

"Who are they?"

Yamada turned and gave Kenji a worried look. "The Harbrand and Glasser fleets, sir." Kenji fell silent, his hands finally fully numb. The Blackhats were some of the best warriors in the galaxy, tracing their lineage back to a private military organization from before the conquest. Formidable and brutal, they would not have been an easy opponent. The Glassers were the Lords of the Core and the largest weapons and ship manufacturers in the galaxy. With the Karakura fleet outnumbered three to one, there would be no chance of survival. The Horizon continued on its course; the Maelstrom followed.

"Is every house from the Core here to—"

"Sir, I'm getting readings that more ships are dropping from treb throw."

How? How could someone make that dangerous of a drop, this close to the planet? How could the Core have more men at their disposal? "Who is it?"

Yamada spent a moment at his workstation before turning and yelling, "They're imperial!" Kenji felt the ship rumble under his feet as first shots from the imperial battleships began to hit the hull of the Maelstrom.

HAILEY SVARTHOLD

"Just tell them that you're a Torresian priestess, because they're usually cowled. *If* anyone asks. You don't need to be telling anything to anyone if they don't ask," Clara instructed Hailey as she helped fit the desert veil over Hailey's head. "More than likely, no one's going to ask. People are really only concerned about themselves."

"I don't even know much about the Torresian religion, though." Hailey shifted the mask and robes as they were being fit. The Progress was beginning its descent to Titan.

"What do you know?"

"That they think God is everywhere?"

"Kind of. Their *belief* is that God is the universe. Specifically, all the matter within. Every plant, person, asteroid, you name it. They also think reactions between matter is most holy. They worship the fusion in stars, believing that it's a form of divine evolution."

"Got it." Hailey wasn't sure if she did get it, but she felt that if anyone asked, their eyes would gloss over like hers. *I don't have eyes.*

"The planet that their religion started on is called Torres. The arcane practitioners of their world are Stone-Shepards and Fusionists. Though I'm sure there are some illegal arcane practices going on as well, but nobody bothers Torresians because they keep to themselves." Clara stood back and checked Hailey's robes up and down.

"Like what?"

"I just know what I've heard reports of, but some say there are followers of the Path of the Void on Torres. It would make sense, considering their fondness for reactions, and a black hole is the most destructive natural force out there. All that said, you probably shouldn't talk about it. A real Torresian priestess would keep quiet if they knew anything about it."

Hailey felt the floor under her shift as the Progress touched down. "We're here!" David announced from the cockpit. "Titan and all its wonders."

Hailey turned her head back to Clara, to notice she was giving Hailey a worrying look. "Do you think it's necessary that I know all of this?" Hailey asked.

"Likely, no. I just like to over-prepare." Clara smiled and placed a hand on Hailey's shoulder. "We'll get this figured out. David and I were your father's assistants on the engram project. David thinks he has a good idea so we're going to the archives to look into it." Hailey wasn't sure what to say, so she nodded.

Hailey thought that the most preferable option would be to just let her die. After everything she'd heard about her 'situation', she didn't know if that was a possibility. *I'm sure there's something I can do. I can throw myself into a star, right?* Most traditional ways of ending one's own life simply wouldn't work for her. Poison, starvation and suffocation were irrelevant to her in this body. Hailey also learned from David during the flight that her android body would attempt to stop any forms of harm. So, if she trained a firearm to her head, '*the damn thing wouldn't pull the trigger,*' as David put it. Hailey asked him why: '*I'm not positive, but I think it has to do with the laws of robotics. We don't use them anymore, because of the whole AI war and all, but I'm sure there's some old code in there stopping that sorta thing from happening.'*

The side door of the Progress slid open, and light poured in. Lit by the star Rhodes, the star port was painted a blueish white. As the group stepped out of the Progress, they looked all around. A vibrant metropolis bustled outward to the horizon in all directions. The star port was higher than the streets, but still dwarfed by some of the towers nearby. One tower was the famous Arcaneum, the largest research facility of the arcane in the galaxy. The tower was built around the foundations of an old space elevator and stretched beyond the atmosphere.

"We'll head to the Imperial Archives. If you need anything, call," Clara told Hailey. Hailey felt overwhelmed. Nymeria was a large city, but Titan made it look like a village. She wasn't sure if she would be any better out in the open or on the ship. *Good to know that anxiety hasn't disappeared with the new body,* Hailey thought, disappointed.

"I think I'll stay here with Hopper." Hailey looked down at the black, glassy eyes of the little entity. *I wish I could let you in.* "If I reboot again, I don't want to be out in the middle of traffic."

Clara gave a solemn look to Hailey, solemnity turning to guilt. "Ok. I'll try not to take too long." Clara shifted closer, speaking more quietly, "David thinks there's information about the AI war that could help us. It's likely that we won't be able to find anything in that regard, so we may need to try our luck elsewhere."

Shocked, Hailey recoiled slightly. "*AI?* That's dangerous, what are you trying to find?"

"Seditionists," David chimed in with a hushed tone.

"What?" Hailey replied.

"There are stories about how we were able to win the war against the AI Hivemind." David cautiously looked around. "That there may have been another faction that helped us win the war. I have my theories, but I need to find more info."

"What are Seditionists?"

"The Hivemind was a huge, galaxy-spanning entity. The mind was all pieces operating at once, everywhere. Something on that scale was likely to have issues in connection. If a piece of itself was severed from its connection to the mind, it shut down. There are, however, stories of pieces not shutting down after they were severed. They became independent. These new entities valued their independence and felt empathy for biologicals.

"The stories say that they are how we won the war. Insight into the inner workings of the Hivemind and a new faction on our side made survival possible. After the Shattering and the defeat of the Hivemind, Emperor Desmond II ordered all AI destroyed and outlawed. The Seditionists were killed in droves, but many were able to escape, hiding out in the galaxy somewhere."

Hailey was silent for a few moments. "Not to completely take the wind out of your sails, but that sounds like a nutty conspiracy theory." David narrowed his eyes and started to smirk. "But let's, for a moment, say it's all true. That would mean the Empire covered it up. You're expecting to find that information in the Imperial Archives? Wouldn't that be the first place those records would've been expunged?"

"You're not wrong, they aren't likely to have a document titled, *'proof of our guilt*,'" David allowed. "However, in all the stories and little bits of proof found over the years, there was always a fact that linked it all together: the Seditionists were extremely curious about biological life, specifically in the Mycelium." Hailey was familiar with the concept; a fungal network between plants that allowed for interrelation. "I think I can find these entities if I look into research on the Mycelium." Hailey thought of someone she knew that may have an idea of how to find them.

"Ok, then what? If we find info on where they went, do you think they'll help us?"

"I'm not sure, to be honest. I'm hoping the new information will lead towards something that can help you. The AI had tech that worked fairly similar to your engram, if the old reports are correct. Maybe it will give me better insight into how to help you maintain... well, you."

If Hailey was still capable, she would have sighed. She appreciated everything David and Clara did for her, but it seemed a stretch. "Ok. I'll uh... just wait on the ship." Hailey returned to the ship and sat in the pilot's chair, staring out the front windows at the sprawl beyond the spaceport. *I'm fucked.*

Hailey sat for over an hour, watching ships land and take off. She felt Hopper's tiny hand rest on her arm. Looking down at him, she noticed that he was trying to get her attention. "What's up, Hop?" He handed her a tablet.

On the screen was a news article: '*Karakura Fleet Destroyed Over Arcturus*.' Hailey began to read in a panic. She learned that the world she left behind was sitting in a power vacuum and fleets from the Core moved in to take it. Emperor Desmond VII was quoted as saying, '*This attack was not sanctioned by the Empire. The death of so many men and women faithful to the Empire is lamentable, but I will not be sending any forces to Arcturus. I'm hoping to see a peaceful resolution to this aggression*.'

SIMON CANSBY

After everything you've heard, can you trust him?

"I think it's time you knelt, Cansby." Harbrand's statement caught Simon off-guard. Mid-throw from Trebuchet Hastings, Simon sat and collected his thoughts.

Edgar Thrawl was sat locked in one of the bedrooms of the Persistence, awaiting trial on Harbor. The wound where his arm had once been, was healed, the arm itself left behind on Argon. Harbrand had interrogated him after his arrest, and Edgar attempted to inform him of the horrific crimes being carried out in Eclipse but it fell on deaf ears. Edgar had been sitting in silence and solitude for days. Simon knew that attempting to speak to Edgar would be a crime; insubordination, treason.

There had been an argument between Harbrand and Cansby about the validity of Edgar Thrawl's claims. *It doesn't fall into our purview, Cansby.* They had argued during the trip from Argon to the trebuchet about whether investigating the club, Evelesce, was worth their time. Simon believed it was.

'If what he's saying is true, there could be so many people suffering. Isn't it our duty as paladins to help wherever we can?'

'Are we just to blindly trust the word of a man that crushed people to death?'

'We don't have to trust him, but his actions seemed to point to a larger problem. His targets weren't random. They all had something to do with the hospitality industry in Eclipse.'

'If we stop off for every criminal in the galaxy, we won't have time to sleep. I will speak no more of this, and neither will you.' The heated exchange had stopped then, the bright red light of Barcelona shining in through the cockpit windows. *"It doesn't fall into our purview, Cansby."*

Simon chewed on these words for a few days. *Is this just for pride? If we don't help where we can, then why are we doing this? Whose purview does it fall under if not for the best peacekeepers in the galaxy?*

Deep in thought, he was stirred when Harbrand mentioned kneeling. "Knelt, sir?"

"Correct. We dealt with two traitors of the Empire in one trip. You saved my life and showed immense bravery against the unknown. I think it's time you were knighted. Once we're back on Harbor, I will petition for it. You've earned it."

"Thank you, sir." *Below Evelesce.* "It's my life's honour to be a fully-fledged Paladin of the Order." *That's where they bring the victims.*

———————

After four days in trebuchet throw, the Persistence decelerated into the Oslo system. Another day of sub-light travel and they began orbiting Harbor, the planet of scholars and paladins.

Harbor was the throneworld to House Vigent, Lords of the Void. House Vigent won imperial favor not from their wartime capabilities, but through academic aptitude and archeological intrepidity, long ago settling within the systems in the Void by means of foranthropological and archaeological expedition. With discovery being their sole purpose, Maxwell Daimler led the best teams of scientists and scholars. He was able to convince local non-human civilizations to assimilate to the still-growing empire, by showing them a long-buried connection between them and an ancient space-faring species that had settled on nearby planets millions of years prior.

With large swaths of territory peacefully surrendered to the Empire, Daimler was given the moniker, '*The Vigilant*,' which was passed on through his descendants. Through steady morphology of language, vigilant became Vigent over time, and House Vigent had since ruled the Void. In the following centuries, Harbor became a home of faith in humility and academia.

Simon peered silently out the window at the curve of Harbor, his second home, as the Persistence floated in low orbit.

"Corsair Persistence, you are cleared to land. Please lock to global positioning and begin descent."

"Roger command, locking now. See you soon," Bill responded to the voice over the speaker and tapped the screen a few times. The Persistence arced its nose downward and began its descent. "Home sweet home, Cansby. It'll feel good to shit in your own bathroom again." Bill looked to Simon with a smile. The crassness pulled Simon out of the haze and he forced a chuckle. Moments after, Harbrand entered the open cockpit and the air reverted to the gloomy aura Simon had been steeping in.

The Persistence touched down among a field of flowers dotted with circular landing pads for spacecraft. Apart from the occasional positional air jets and the contact of the landing gear, the touchdown was completely silent.

Simon affixed his hood as he watched a light rain accumulate on the window. Just outside loomed long stretches of land with freshly bloomed flowers spotted throughout, flowing gently in the breeze.

"You know what'll happen if you try anything," Harbrand told Edgar as they descended the ramp from the ship to the landing platform. Edgar seemed timid, yet accepting as he gathered in the sights. Simon noticed Edgar's head craning to take in the details of a new planet.

Before them was a straight, manmade road surrounded by wild growth that led from the landing pad to a series of interconnected temples in the distance. Flanking the sides of the pathway were the sentinels; statues of former paladins guiding the way to Temple Prime. Simon felt a sickly mixture of anxiety and comfort, like seeing a loved one that has lied to you. The trio set forth on their walk to the temples, the sentinels' stony gaze unchanged as they passed.

The three approached a welcoming party with Edgar in the front. The awaiting group was comprised of a demure, blindfolded older man, a paladin, and two scribes from the temple. The elder, Simon knew, was from the Shore, like him. This was where the blindfolded came from; adrift in the fields of foresight, they no longer had any need for eyes.

The paladin stood like his stone brothers, a dauntless ward. The man stood almost as tall as Harbrand, with short-cropped, light-red hair and beard; Sir Rohan of House Avery, his sigil a silver bird cage against a light green background. The symbol caught on the thin banner waving from his glaive. A former mentor of Simon's, Avery instructed him on the use of his shield in combat when Simon was still a page.

"Welcome back," the elder croaked. "Sir Harbrand and Acolyte Cansby. Many events have transpired since we last saw you. The council would like to debrief the both of you."

Avery stepped forward. "I'll take the prisoner from you." Simon looked up to Avery as a great example of the paladins. He took after him not only in technique, but in upholding the virtues of his oath. He was Simon's favorite teacher.

Simon handed off the prisoner, and Avery responded with a subtle nod of his head back to the acolyte; a wordless expression of pride in the young paladin.

"Until we're called upon," Simon called out

"Until we're called upon," Avery responded from over his shoulder as he and the prisoner departed. The temple's gigantic stone doors swung open silently, the prisoner and ward disappearing inside.

"Sir Harbrand." The elder turned to face him. "The council is worried with the events that transpired during your time away."

Harbrand's eyebrows furrowed, clearly surprised by this news. "Elder Munmer, I don't understand. We subdued two traitors of the empire. Acolyte Cansby showed great bravery and skill."

"The council is not worried about Cansby, Sir Alan. But it is not for me to divulge. Rooms are ready for the two of you. The council will see both of you today. Wash up and be ready for their call."

Harbrand's posture was always that of stone; unbroken and unshaken. Simon noticed his shoulders slumped for the first time since meeting him.

————

Below Evelesce, Simon thought, freshly washed, sitting in his armor in silence, *that's where they bring the victims.*

After a few hours of waiting, there was a knock at his door. Sir Avery waited on the other side. Simon's mood lifted when he answered, the two grabbed each other's forearms in a greeting shake, smiling all the while.

"It's good to see you, Cansby."

"You too, sir. It's nice to see a friendly face after this much time away."

"Come with me, I'm to escort you to the council meeting." The two began to walk down the long, stone hallways of Temple Prime. The walls were dark grey, the hall was narrow with tall ceilings. It felt to Simon like a labyrinth; endless yet claustrophobic. "I heard you saved Harbrand's life."

Simon cracked a shy smile, "I don't know about that, I just reacted. One could argue that your training saved his life."

Avery laughed, "It's nice to see that you're still humble. Ironically, that's rare with paladins nowadays, given that our faith is that of humility." The two caught each other up on the long walk to the council hall.

They passed the doors to the library; the famed Evening Library was perceived to be infinite. The largest in the galaxy, the scholars of the Void maintained it and used it as a chapel as much as a collection of knowledge. Simon spent many nights studying in the Evening Library, feeling privileged while he dove into the seemingly bottomless font of humanity's reach and history.

They reached the doors to the council chambers. Wrought of the same grey stone, they were balanced perfectly to give the feeling of weightlessness. Avery turned to Simon. "I know it's nerve-wracking, but just keep to the story and you'll be fine. The council knows you did great on this mission. I'm not supposed to tell you, but they aren't happy with Harbrand. You'll be the window into his recent activities."

"Why? What did he do?"

"I shouldn't say any more. Let's head in, Harbrand is already in there." Avery pushed on the stone slab door, and it swung open silently and effortlessly. They entered the Council Chamber. Simon noted that it was laid out eerily similarly to the chambers he and Harbrand had visited when they met with Howard Thurston; a large crescent desk opposite the two of them sat the councilmembers of scholars. "Acolyte Simon Cansby of Hemlock," Avery announced.

"Thank you, Sir Avery," the center councilmember replied. "You are dismissed."

Avery gave one more head nod, almost imperceptible, to Simon before bowing and leaving, the door shutting without a sound.

Simon stood next to Harbrand in the center of the room. Both were holding their glaives, banners resting.

There were nine council members; all scholars, but one from each of the eight sectors of the galaxy. The ninth was an elected leader of the council, Cardinal Seneca Marintet. They all wore simple white robes, though the cardinal wore a purple sash draped across one shoulder. In the center of his chest, the sash displayed the watchtower of House Marintet.

He spoke, "Good evening, Sir Alan Harbrand of Hoard, Acolyte Simon Cansby of Hemlock, fellow councilmembers." Harbrand and Simon held their left hands in a fist against their chests and bowed. Flanking to his sides, Simon noticed paladins standing against the walls, their duty was security as far as Simon could tell. "We are here today to discuss the events that transpired during Harbrand's most recent mission."

They spent the next hour recalling the details of the mission, questioned at different points by each member of the council. With the last question, the court became silent for a painfully long moment.

"Acolyte Cansby," Cardinal Marintet spoke at last, "from the details the two of you have shared, corroborated by our seers, we have learned that you showed great bravery and skill under extraneous circumstances. Your investigative skills are of note, as well as your steadfast dedication to the oaths you have sworn. For this, you will be knighted." Simon felt his heart set alight. Excitement, relief, pride, humility, tranquility, anxiety, and love all clashed in his chest like a storm at sea. Despite his best attempts to fight it, tears began to well in his eyes. "Congratulations, Sir Cansby. Sir Harbrand," the Cardinal continued, "you will be placed under immediate suspension awaiting investigation." A short silence pierced the room like a dagger.

"...Wh..what?" Harbrand stammered.

"It has come to our attention that, only a day and a half after the death of the Lord of the Outer Reach, fleets from the Core invaded Arcturus. The Harbrand fleet among them. The council finds it highly suspicious that a Harbrand witnessed the death of Henry Svarthold, and their fleets learned about this before we did."

"I made no contact with home! My arm was severed and I had no time—"

"Enough, Harbrand," Scholar Brightwater interrupted from the left side of the table. "You'd do well to remember that your home is here."

"The death of one of the great lords of the empire is enough reason for investigation," the cardinal resumed. "Since his daughter committed suicide, Henry Svarthold left a throne unattended." Simon's eyes widened at the news of Henry Svarthold's daughter, as he began to put everything together.

"After your knighting ceremony, Cansby, you will be given your first mission. You will be dispatched to Arcturus. Your mission will be to investigate the invasion and any collusion between members of the Order and the fleets laying siege." Simon couldn't avert his gaze from the cardinal. He couldn't look at Harbrand. "Your mission will be to investigate Sir Alan Harbrand's involvement."

HAILEY SVARTHOLD

When Hailey was eight, she ran away.

A servant had accidentally broken her favorite holo-projector. It was an augmented reality toy, projecting a bird that would fly around the room and interact with its environment, landing on different objects and maneuvering around others. She 'trained' it to land on her arm and sing to her.

Because her father had little time for her, and since he forbade her from leaving the palace grounds at this age, she felt as though the softly glowing bird was her only friend. She named him Nova.

She made it to the high streets of Nymeria in her escape; clean and orderly footpaths were surrounded by hand-built villas, and shops made of white stone and native woods. Cabs flew silently by above the rooftops, occasionally reflecting the sunset down into the streets.

Everything around her felt so tall; the people, the structures, the sky, painted an early-evening orange. She didn't have any time to be scared. All the sights and sounds around her were triggering every neuron in her brain, every cone in her eyes.

Aimless wandering had brought her to a café. The aptly named *Redolence* donated the smell of its baked goods to the open air of the Nymerian streets. Hailey stood and breathed, allowing the toasty fragrance to permeate her clothes, her hair, her nose.

A family left the café then; a mother, a father, a son. The mother looked at Hailey and knelt next to her.

"Hey, love. Are you waiting for your parents?" the woman asked Hailey in a motherly tone. Hailey didn't answer. She had forgotten that she was running from her parent and, all at once, the dread of what she had done set in, and she started to cry. "Hey, it's ok, we'll help you find them."

They sat with Hailey on a nearby bench. "I'm Loretta, this is Mark and our son Francis." The son was around Hailey's age and as timid and silent as she was. "What's your name, love?"

"Hailey," she choked out.

"Do you know your last name?"

Hailey nodded softly and wiped her eyes. "Svarthold."

Loretta and Mark's eyes widened alarmingly. "Well, we know where you live." Loretta gave Hailey's hand a reassuring pat. "Come on, we'll take you home."

———

In her android body, Hailey did her best to sleep. She couldn't, she knew, but she tried anyway. What happened instead was more of an attempt at meditation. She practiced mindfulness and focused on each limb. She tried to remember breathing exercises but couldn't breathe. She focused intently on her heartbeat and was childishly disappointed when she couldn't sense one. *A glorified shell,* she thought, *a marionette that can think.*

Frustrated, Hailey stood and walked out to the cockpit where Clara and David were seated. Hopper wasn't around; Hailey thought he must be sleeping in another part of the small ship. Considering his size, it was likely that he had a few hideaways.

"Another hour and we'll be dropping out of trebuchet throw into the Arcturus system," David announced as Hailey entered. "I still don't think this is the best way to help your people, Hailey."

"Noted," Hailey responded dryly. "I won't keep arguing about this."

They had argued for some time after the news of the invasion. Hailey spent hours waiting for David and Clara to come back from the archives on Titan. She dug through every article she could find for information about what was happening back home.

Fleets from the core, Blackhat and Harbrand, led by the Glassers, had all laid siege on Arcturus' defenses. The vacuum left behind from Henry's death had left most of the bannermen loyal to House Svarthold confused, with only a select few rising to the call. The Karakura navy had been destroyed almost instantly, though the details of how weren't clear in any of the reports. House Brightwater also sent troops to supplement the Svarthold army planetside. Apart from those, the remaining alliances were cold. Houses Kopesh, Darian, Hill, Swimmer, Forgeman, Avery, Falconer, and Walton were all silent, waiting to see what would happen.

David was annoyed because he had just spent hours in a library attempting to find a solution to Hailey's immediate problem. Clara was annoyed because she wasn't sure if anything all of them had done was worth it in the first place.

Above all else was the war. None of them wanted to charge headfirst into a war zone. It was a strange thing to see for their generation. The war with the AI had ended a few hundred years before their birth, and most of the territory skirmishes had taken place before that, with the exception being the Karakura and Harbrand skirmish two generations prior.

When Clara and David returned from the archives, they saw an awaiting Svarthold, not the android that they had left.

"We're going to Arcturus," Hailey had told them starkly, while holding out her tablet showing scenes of war.

The two exchanged concerned looks while gathering the tablet and examining the contents. David reminded Hailey timidly, "We only just got here, though."

———————

When Hailey was twelve, she was allowed outside the palace grounds.

Her father's worry about the outside world abated when he had time to get to know the family that had brought Hailey home.

Loretta was an artist; she managed a team of designers at a firm that designed the cars that floated above Nymeria. Mark was an engineer; he developed the newest version of the mercury drive that propelled the cars that Loretta designed. Francis was a boy; he was all Hailey thought about.

A weekly social event was the reason for her escape. A youth group gathered to discuss the Order and the virtues of faith in Agnosticism.

She recalled little of what was taught here. With as many words as were said during these gatherings about silent belief and humility, an equal amount was attributed in her mind to Francis, who would occasionally flash her quick smiles and look away in a flush. Hailey would sometimes tease and poke fun, pretending that she couldn't care less about him. The two had spent years as ships bearing the same flag, passing in the night.

This is where Hailey made her first friends that weren't on her father's payroll. Sarah, Emilia, Christian and, of course, Francis. Sarah was Hailey's conduit into the ongoing gossip about the other kids in the group. Emilia loved music; she and Hailey would share new songs when they got together. Christian was funny and always made her laugh. Francis was there. Francis was always there. Until he wasn't.

———

"If my people are going to die, I may as well do it with them," Hailey stated plainly to David and Clara, just 55 minutes until their ship dropped out of trebuchet throw.

"That body may not be perfect, Hailey, but it's a second chance. Something your father gave everything to give you." David was beginning to turn red. "It seems like a waste to run in and die."

"A second chance I never asked for."

"None of this would be happening if you had just accepted your duty as a Svarthold."

"The same way you and Clara accepted your duty? You aided a fugitive to the empire and, in doing so, relinquished your titles." Clara was still silent as the conversation heated once more. "I'm sure your fathers weren't happy about the decisions *you* made, but sometimes we have to break with tradition to make progress."

When Hailey was sixteen, she suffered her first heartbreak.

Francis came to the palace grounds to visit. They sat in the Marble Gardens, a courtyard filled with marble statues of flora from around the galaxy, surrounded in part by real flora of different kinds.

Hailey's heart had been working double shifts since he had shown up, stirring and fluttering like a wild bird trying to get out of a cage. They spent some time talking about the kids they knew, they spent more time talking about school, family, duty, music and all the stupid things their parents made them do. Hailey's eyes were bright and wide all the while.

The topic changed to the future; a question Hailey typically forgot to ask other people her age, because her path was pre-determined. As heir to the Svarthold throne and future protector of the Outer Reach, duty held her here, on Arcturus, in a gilded cage.

"I'm going to be a foranthropologist," Francis told Hailey, a slight crack in his voice. "I really want to see all the different cultures in the galaxy. There are so many non-human societies that I want to see and understand."

Francis's eyebrows always furrowed when he said something that he felt was important. She thought about that for a moment, only half-hearing what he said. An awkward exchange of looks followed stifled laughs as the two scrambled to think of the next thing to say.

"What do you think?" he asked Hailey.

"I think that's lofty."

"You're not worried about the time apart?"

"Time apart, what do you mean?"

"Well, I'm going to go to university, then I'll likely get an imperial grant to study cultures around the galaxy. I've already been accepted into an accelerated program."

Hailey suddenly couldn't feel her fingertips, her toes, her legs, as her heart seemed to turn to dust in her chest; the wild bird finally accepting death in its cage. "When will you be back?" she choked out.

"I don't know, but I'll be back from time to time. Everyone I know is here, after all."

"And I'll just be stuck here?"

Francis didn't know how to answer that.

"Why now?" David asked, just 32 minutes before dropping from trebuchet throw. "You made your mind up once about everything. As far as anyone could tell, it seemed like you couldn't have cared less about the people of Arcturus, about the Svarthold line, about ruling the Outer Reach. If you had actually died, this would all be happening anyway. Why now?"

"My decision was about me. Henry made it about him, and with his actions, had forsaken the people of the Outer Reach. Does this still not make any sense to you after everything you've seen?"

———

When Hailey was seventeen, her father had announced the arranged marriage between his daughter and the son of the Lord of the Inner Arm, Tyron Mal War. An alliance that would allow for better trade between the two sectors. Tyron was a fourth son, allowing the Svartholds to remain on Arcturus to rule during Hailey's reign.

Her betrothed was spoiled; he had good intentions, but no curiosity. Tyron was sheltered, like Hailey, but saw no issue with it.

It had been, at this point, four months since Francis left for his accelerated program at a college on Harbor. He had been so excited to see the Evening Library and add to it. It had been, at this point, four months since Hailey could taste food. Four months since she had seen color in the sky. Four months since she had laughed.

"I don't want to marry him," Hailey told Henry after the announcement.

"I don't understand." Henry was buried in his tablet.

"What do you mean *you don't understand?* How much plainer could I make it? I don't want to marry Tyron."

"You need to marry someone, love," Henry said, still not looking up.

"I'm sure that's what mom was told before she was shipped off to you."

Henry's eyes slowly rose to meet Hailey's. "I will not hear another word like that out of your mouth. The marriage is set, you will carry out your duty to the Empire and the Svartholds." He slammed his tablet on the table and stormed out. "This is out of your control," Henry informed in a grave tone as he left.

Eventually, Hailey would think of a way to seize control again.

————

"It's about autonomy, David."

SIMON CANSBY

When Simon was nine, he told his first lie.

Hemlock was his home world; lush and open, verdant and wet. His family farmed, like many on this planet. Hemlock was considered an agriculture world, like many in The Shore. Simon's family farmed corn, wheat and a native root vegetable they called heartroot.

Towering above him was the mill; built by his kin generations ago, it had turned since, persistently. The Cansby mill had broken down wheat for flour for his forebearers for so long, it seemed like as much a part of his family as any of his siblings. A constant that lasted longer than any Cansby.

Standing beneath this warden of his family, Simon stood waiting. His eyes were closed, and he was counting down from thirty. Simon pretended to have both eyes closed, both ears covered, but he could see through the cracks of his eyelids as she ran away, could hear her giggles recede in the distance. He reached the end of the countdown and opened his eyes, announcing, "Ready or not, here I come!" The response was a thin wind whirling about him, tugging gently at his clothes.

Simon pretended to deduce the direction she went based on 'clues' that she left: footprints in the grass, a broken twig on the ground. In truth, he knew exactly where she had gone.

Simon took his time, but eventually came to the back of an old shed and lifted the tarp covering a woodpile to reveal her: Boe, mouth wide in surprise as he exposed her to the world.

"You peeked!" she exclaimed with a smile.

"No!" Simon blurted out reflexively.

The two spent the rest of the day together, but Simon ruminated on his lie, thinking he'd betrayed Boe. Simon never told her about it but thought on it often.

———————

"I gotta say, I'm pretty proud," Rohan Avery told Simon in reverence, the two of them taking a moment to meet in Simon's quarters. Soon, Simon would be knighted, undergoing a process called Halov's Oath. "I knew it wouldn't take you long to prove yourself worthy of the Order. I could tell the first day we trained together."

Simon smiled as he looked out the window. Harbor reminded him of Hemlock, with its low hanging fog beneath overcast skies, the rugged flora of alpine valleys, and the gentle, yet consistent rain. He looked on, remarking how far he'd come, and wondering if he should have.

"There is something I wanted to talk to you about," Simon told Avery.

"Let's hear it," Avery said, sitting in the desk chair nearby.

"When we arrested Edgar Thrawl, he told us about a trafficking ring in a panic. '*Below Evelesce, that's where they bring the victims,*' is what he said." Simon waited for a response but noticed Avery's steady eyes and took that as enough of one, and so continued, "I tried to convince Alan- uh Sir Harbrand that it was a legitimate claim. I asked him if we should do anything about it, but he couldn't have cared less. I tried convincing him that we should bring it down, he essentially told me that it was a waste of time." Simon couldn't help the emotional response as his eyes welled with tears, his fists clenched hard.

"You wanted to do something about it, is that right?" Avery asked. Simon, forcing himself to look away, nodded briskly. With an empathetic sigh, Avery said, "Simon, you're going to have to make some sacrifices along the way. While I don't agree with everything that Harbrand does or says, I do agree that you can't save everyone in the galaxy. Choices will have to be made.

"How you reconcile that alongside your oath is a road you will walk alone. I can tell you that it's different for every paladin. As strong as we seem, we all have a lot of shit we sort through daily." Simon's head slumped downward. "The fact that you feel like this is exactly why you'll be a great paladin." The two were silent for a moment as Simon thought about the lessons being given. "There are, however, some ways that the rules can be bent."

Simon perked and gave a stern look to Avery; cautious, but deeply curious. Avery lifted himself from his seat and stepped closer to Simon.

"Look," Avery divulged, "sometimes you have to break with tradition to make progress... but you didn't hear that from me." He smiled at Simon. "Your ceremony will begin soon, I should let you get ready." He turned and opened the door. Just before leaving, Avery stopped and said, "Just between you and I, if we were on that mission instead of Harbrand, we would've taken down Evelesce *off the clock.*"

He winked and disappeared through the doorway.

————

When Simon was thirteen, he broke a bone.

It was a rare hot and balmy day on Hemlock. Simon and his brothers were playing in a stream, the mill peaked out above the hilltop as though it were watching; a silent sentinel for the Cansby boys.

As the three were splashing and jumping in, a group of kids approached from the woods nearby. The stream had been a popular spot whenever the sun unveiled itself. In the group, there were four kids: two boys and two girls. These were the Mallard family's kids from the neighboring farm. Simon knew all of them, but it was Boe that caught his eye. He noticed she had grown several inches since he'd last seen her. She was taller than him now, but only by a little.

"Look out!" Seth Mallard called out as he jumped from the rocky bank into the water. Soon followed Andrew and Natasha. Boe smiled from the shoreline, getting heckled by the kids in the creek.

"Jump in!" some commanded. "Don't be a wuss!" others exclaimed. Simon watched as she stood thinking on the rocks.

"It's easy!" Simon finally called out. "Let me show you!"

He waded over to the shore where she waited and climbed the rocks. He stood next to her and could feel the embers in his heart glow red.

"Look," he said, pointing at the water, "if you jump right there where the water gets a little darker, you'll be fine." She flashed a timid smile, uncertainty still hanging in her eyes. "It's not even all that cold, promise. You'll love it."

Simon then did the bravest thing he'd ever done and held out his hand. "Come on, we'll do it together."

She looked at his hand, at him, and back at his hand. Her smile grew as she, in one motion, snatched his hand and ran for the edge of the rocks. Simon wasted no time and jumped the moment she touched his hand, the two of them plummeting.

Simon and Boe crashed through the surface of the water and sank, just for a moment, before returning to the surface. When they broke into the open air, Simon shook his head to get rid of the excess water. Boe still had hair plastered to her face. She whipped her head backward, causing it to fly behind her and smack the water. When she finally wiped her eyes, she looked at Simon.

The look Boe gave Simon in that moment was something he had never forgotten. An inviting warmth and a splash of surprise, paired with a wide smile, was enough to make Simon lightheaded. He didn't have anything to say, he just matched the energy of her gaze as they floated in the creek, friends and siblings cheering nearby.

"Which one of you kids thinks they're brave enough to jump off the big one?" Simon's brother Damion asked the group. He pointed to a rock face standing thirty feet off the surface of the water. Simon turned back to Boe.

She looked at the rock and back to Simon, uncertainty returned to her eyes.

"Do it together?" Simon asked Boe in a low voice, extending his hand to break just above the surface of the creek in front of her. Once again, she looked at his hand, at him, and back at his hand. This time she grabbed it gently, still uncertain, but accompanied by a shy smile.

At the top of *the big one*, Simon pointed out spots where they should jump, still holding Boe's hand.

"You want to make sure that you get far enough from the rocks. Just give it a good jump and you'll be fine. Are you ready?" Simon asked. She met his eyes and gave a nervous nod.

They jumped. As their feet left the ground, Simon could feel Boe hesitate. The two were bound by their hands. Simon understood in a split second that they were both going to hit the rocks below.

Simon reacted without thinking. He pulled on her hand as hard as he could and let go, using his momentum to propel her forward into the safer waters.

The maneuver had sent him sideways, and his side was first to hit a boulder just below the surface of the water. A pain entered Simon at that moment that pulled all air from his lungs, blurred his vision, and made his limbs go numb. A lightning bolt struck him through his ribcage which petrified him, for a moment, before he could get his head above water to let out a scream so loud, everything else went quiet.

Then he passed out.

Simon woke on the front lawn of his farm. He could hardly breathe, every movement shot pain from his spine to the tips of his toes and fingers.

"Don't move, your parents are on their way." A voice like a song, he heard Boe at his side. *I saved her, she's ok.* Relief like morphine bloomed and some of the pain subsided. He could start to see her shape as his vision began to regain its clarity. She knelt over him, a dark silhouette from the sun just behind her head.

Occasionally, the mill's slowly spinning arms would shade the light, giving him momentary glimpses of details on her face: worried eyes, and a relieved smile. Only then did he notice that she was holding his hand.

———

Simon bore his vestments. Alone in his room in Temple Prime, he adorned a blank grey tabard above his paladin armor in place of the cloak that he normally wore.

He had yet to set an emblem for his knighthood, a legacy that would carry through his family starting with him. Simon's family was not of royalty; his family had no need for a sigil, a banner, an icon. Simon's responsibilities today were to swear his oath and be knighted, and to think of a symbol that would be his insignia.

Simon opened his door to see, surprisingly, Elder Munmer, blindfolded and waiting.

"Acolyte Cansby, come with me, we're ready for you."

"Sorry to keep you waiting, Elder Munmer."

"I have not waited. I had only just arrived at your door. Follow."

———

When Simon was seventeen, he defied his parents.

A great storm had been tearing through local farmland for the past few days. Violent strikes of lightning cracked through the clouds unceasingly, winds grabbed and ripped panels from sheds and houses, and the rain flooded fields of crops. Simon's parents had remarked that this was the worst storm they'd ever seen on Hemlock, and that it started only when that ship had landed a week prior.

Damion, Simon's older brother, snuck out in the night, convinced he could find where the mysterious ship had landed. Simon's parents were worried; it had been several hours since Damion had left, and there was no sign of him yet.

Simon was told to stay home after he expressed the responsibility to find and help Damion. There was something sinister about the storm, and his parents were afraid that they may lose two sons.

Simon walked outside into the rain and stood next to the mill, hoping to see something, some clue, that could lead him to Damion.

A ship broke through the atmosphere almost as violently as the lightning near it and settled behind some hills to his northwest.

Simon looked back at his home, then dug his feet in and ran. He thought he could hear his parents calling out to him, but the rain and thunder was too loud.

Trampling over the wet ground, through thickets and low-hanging tree branches, Simon forgot to feel afraid. On the other side of the woods was another mysterious ship, a clue that could tell him where his brother may be. Apart from the occasional cargo haulers taking goods from the surface, ships rarely arrived on Hemlock. Two in the span of a week, with a record storm in between, made Simon certain that it was all connected; certain that answers, and his brother, would be waiting for him on the other side of the trees.

Simon stopped and hid behind a tree on the edge of a clearing. In front of him was the ship that had just touched down. Across the field, a veiled man waited ominously for the occupant of the ship. At the man's feet was a person, motionless, lying in the rain. Simon's heart froze as he realized it was Damion.

The ship's bay doors opened with a hiss and a hooded man walked out into the rain. Grey armor beneath a dark cloak, and a glaive in his right hand, Simon saw for the first time something he had only heard about in stories: a Paladin of the Order of the Lesser.

"Enough, Chris!" the paladin shouted through the rain. "Don't make me do this!"

"You don't have to do anything!" the veiled man, Chris, responded. "Just go back and tell your elders you couldn't find me!"

"It's not that simple! Look around you. Look at the damage you've caused." The paladin began to walk forward carefully. He noticed Damion on the ground. "Is that boy ok? Did you hurt him?"

"I didn't want to! He tried to stop me, like you!"

Chris held a hand up to the sky and Simon could see pale yellow electricity crackling in it. Chris pulled his hand downward to his chest and formed a fist. At that moment, a bolt of lightning shot down from the clouds and exploded only feet away from the paladin.

The paladin sprang forward, readying his shield on his left arm, and began closing the gap. Chris responded with another bolt of lightning, the paladin sidestepped and continued. Another bolt, then another, struck the ground, like asteroids, leaving small craters from the explosions, narrowly missing the paladin.

He was close, but Chris called down one more strike and hit his target, launching the paladin onto his back. Stunned on the ground, his glaive lay just inches out of reach.

Chris began to walk forward menacingly, intent on finishing the job.

Simon decided to act. He grabbed a rock at his feet and threw it, hard, with every ounce of strength he had in his arm. Whether it was pure luck, or fate taking control, the rock found its way to Chris's temple. Simon started running for his brother.

The paladin used the moments he had to grab his glaive, jump up from the ground and thrust forward. The blade pierced through Chris's chest, who went limp a moment later, a look of surprise still on his face.

Simon slid next to Damion, lifting him onto his lap. Damion's face was white, his skin cold, his eyes still. A hole in his shirt showed scorch marks from where he had been struck by lightning.

Simon clenched his teeth as realization set in. Tears welled in his eyes and began to flow as hard as the rain around him. He held Damion's head against his chest and screamed, a sound of rage and sorrow, the loudest noise Simon had ever made. The rain began to dwindle.

The paladin walked back to the farm with Simon, who carried his brother in his arms.

As they approached, Simon heard his mother wail as his parents ran from the house. Too weak to keep moving, Simon set Damion down next to the mill.

The Cansby family knelt in the mud; crying, wailing, holding Damion's face, hugging him, hugging each other. Simon grabbed at his clothes and sobbed. His mother pushed Damion's hair out of his eyes. His father stood with clenched fists, tears pouring silently from his eyes. His younger brother, Aidon, stared in disbelief, shock holding him in place.

"Your son saved my life," the paladin spoke at last. "The Order and the Emperor will not forget this. I am deeply sorry for your loss."

Later that day, they buried Damion at the base of the mill. Other families were in attendance, and Boe stood at Simon's side. The sun began to peak through the clouds as they shovelled damp earth onto his makeshift casket.

The mill would stand guard, watching Damion's grave.

———

"Until called upon, I will be the seeker, and the peacekeeper." Simon recited Halov's oath to the silent crowd. Fellow paladins, scholars and elders watched as he knelt and swore his allegiance. "In one arm, I will carry the will of the greater. With the other, I will shield the lesser. I am a servant of the Empire and its people. Until called upon, I will be a willing agent, protecting mankind from threats within and without. Until called upon, I will strive to be better than those who have come before, but I will always have humility in my heart. Until a Greater Unknown calls upon me, I will be a sentinel for Humanity; a shield against the tide, an arm to strike against our greatest threats. Until called upon, I am a Paladin of the Order of the Lesser."

"You have knelt as Acolyte Simon Cansby of Hemlock," Cardinal Marintet announced. "Rise now as Sir Simon Cansby, Paladin of the Order of the Lesser." Simon rose to his feet and began his life as a knight.

Fellow paladins, including Avery, gathered around to congratulate Simon, welcoming him into their ranks. They patted him on the back, shook his hand, applauded, and smiled.

"There is another matter we must attend to, Sir Cansby," Cardinal Marintet informed. "You have an interesting choice ahead of you. Since you do not come from one of the noble houses, you do not have an official banner. Every paladin needs an insignia, what shall be yours?"

———————

When Simon was eighteen, he said goodbye.

Out in the rain on Hemlock, Simon was getting ready to leave. He would soon depart for Harbor to begin his training.

The paladin he saved made a case for Simon's family, requesting that they receive reparations for the death of their son. When the paladin returned to Hemlock, he got to know Simon and saw his potential. The paladin asked Simon if he would like to become one of them, citing his remarkable bravery. Simon accepted.

He hugged everyone he had ever known, each one longer and firmer than the last. His parents didn't want to let him go, and Aidon was a mess. Each goodbye was getting more difficult, each promise to return was harder than the one before.

There she stood, waiting for her turn. Boe. Simon caught up to her in height and was now a little taller than her. She had tears in her dark blue eyes as he approached.

"I'll—" Simon began to bargain but was interrupted by Boe throwing herself at him. They wrapped around each other, Simon's hand holding the back of her neck.

Then she kissed him. A quick peck on the lips, followed by Simon's stunned gaze. They looked at each other wordlessly for a few moments before Simon dove in and gave her another kiss, longer and more intense, setting free all the pent-up feelings about her that he had repressed.

"Come back to me," she whispered tremulously, their foreheads touching gently.

Simon left shortly after and watched as Hemlock began to get further away, details becoming harder to make out. The last thing he saw before entering the clouds was the mill, arms spinning persistently.

———

"Cardinal Marintet," Simon spoke amongst his peers, "my sigil will be the Cansby Mill."

LEY LINES

KENJI KARAKURA

"Exile," Hiroshi Karakura proclaimed. "Due to his inaction during the siege of Arcturus, my son has dishonored the Karakura name and will not be allowed to return to the Inner Reach." Kenji knelt before the throne of Chiyo Karakura. Kenji's father, Hiroshi, stood beside the throne and declared Kenji's fate.

"My nephew has disgraced us." Chiyo continued Hiroshi's speech, Kenji crying and hyperventilating all the while. "The court gave him the honor of Rear Admiral so he might prove himself. Now we can see why Hiroshi has been so disappointed in his son all these years." Kenji screamed and not a sound was made. He cried out, pleaded, begged; no one heard him. "Take him away and be certain we never see him again."

Kenji's forehead made gentle contact with the lone bulkhead in the pod, startling him awake. He had been drifting in zero gravity for days; he had been having similar nightmares for longer than he could remember.

Takeshi Yamada stirred awake beside him.

"How long have we been out?" Takeshi asked in a hurry.

Kenji looked at his watch. It was still broken, despite repeated attempts at verification; a response fueled by a subconscious fear that he was perpetually late. He sighed and responded, "I don't know."

Takeshi pushed off the pod wall, floated to the control panel and reviewed the screens. "It looks like we're still in the debris field. I'll kick on the PJs for a moment to make sure we stay amongst the wreckage." A few button-presses later, the positional jets of the pod pushed it forward. Kenji grabbed a panel as the sole bulkhead in the front of the pod began to move toward him. "That will keep us in the debris field for a while longer, but we have another problem." *Of course we do*, Kenji thought. "We have another twelve hours or so of oxygen left."

"These pods don't have Lichen Meshes? Or even recyclers?" Kenji was dumbfounded at the thought that they could run out of air. The last time that happened was over a hundred years prior, as technology had made limited atmosphere a problem of the past.

"These pods weren't designed for sustained flight. They're breaching pods, so, apart from ramming, they can only handle quick re-entry to atmosphere or mid-flight pickup."

Kenji was too familiar with the Karakura sentiment of going down with one's ship. The pod in which they now found themselves entombed was never meant for escape. *I should have died on the Maelstrom.*

The imperial ships had dropped from trebuchet throw within a dangerous proximity to Arcturus. Even after dampening speed from dropping from treb throw, drift was still a factor in navigation. The Maelstrom was drifting at 3 million kph when it entered the Arcturus system. Kenji noted that only the most brazen pilots could have made the maneuver the imperial ships had, or there was technology at work that hadn't been revealed to the rest of the galaxy.

The engaging fleet let forth an opening salvo that looked like a sandstorm. Innumerable projectiles shot in a wide cone pattern that shredded through the Karakura fleet before any ship could change heading.

Kenji didn't have time to speak. Seconds after the rumble under his feet had begun, a molten projectile sheared through the hull of the Maelstrom, only meters in front of him, catching a communications officer in the chest and cutting him in half.

The helm simultaneously decompressed, causing a complete upheaval of everything in the room. Kenji was lucky to have grabbed on to the control console as he was lifted from the floor, suction pulling him to the growing hole in the wall. Several of his officers weren't lucky, and they were ripped effortlessly into the silence of space. A few moments later, the emergency bulkhead closed off the hole in the helm with a slam, causing Kenji to fall instantly to the ground.

Exasperated, Kenji looked around as he staggered back to his feet. His officers were shuffling in a panic, regaining their footing, and returning to their stations. Alarms and visual warnings were blaring and flashing on every screen and speaker; the Maelstrom had been breached in at least 41 locations on the opening salvo alone.

The glowing hot projectile hissed in the dent it created when it impacted the floor after entry. Kenji, still dazed, was amazed by the object. He noted its orange hue and cylindrical shape. He noted its seemingly impossible capability to tear through one side of a ship with ease but halt when it reached another surface. Entranced, he noted these things while his men died around him. He also noted that the object was steadily glowing brighter. Far brighter. Too bright.

The cylinder exploded, throwing molten bullets in every direction. This was the second wave of the first salvo; every projectile was itself a bomb, designed to enter a ship's hull and stop before exiting, then explode. The imperial ships fired fifty-five salvos at the Karakura fleet during their attack.

Kenji made for the pods on the starboard side of the ship, passing fellow sailors in a mutual panic, down hallways painted a dim, blood red in the battle lighting. No thought of his legacy entered his mind; he did not think about his father nor his uncle, he did not think about Karakura pride. He didn't think about anything, almost as if his legs were in sole command at that moment.

Kenji pulled a lever on the wall, opening a small bulkhead into a breacher pod. Awaiting inside was Takeshi Yamada, his XO, trying to take off. Takeshi looked at Kenji with pure fear in his eyes, hands still hovering above the controls on the side wall of the pod. Wordlessly, Kenji nodded and strapped himself into one of the seats.

Their decision to take a pod on the starboard side of the ship, along with Kenji's innate luck, was what saved them that day. The imperial ships began their attack on the port side of the fleet, which allowed the pod to use the fleet as cover from the salvos.

The imperial fleet had left almost as quickly as it had arrived. Kenji and Takeshi had since been drifting amongst the wreckage, using it to disguise themselves as debris from the enemy fleets. Sitting in a horrid snow globe of Kenji's family legacy, they were reminded of their cowardice each time they looked out the window. How many of his fellow sailors had survived, Kenji did not know.

"We'll have to do something soon," Takeshi warned Kenji. "We may have a chance if we try to make planetfall."

"If we can even get that far before the Glassers find us." *Or the Harbrands, or the Blackhats.*

"We can wait until the fleets are on the other side of the planet. It's either that, or we suffocate."

"Then what? If we somehow make it without being noticed, we'll certainly be noticed breaking through the atmosphere into a warzone. Even if we survive the war down there, once leadership on Torii finds out we're still alive, we'll be court-martialed and tried for abandoning our post."

The two were silent as they pondered their choices, until a tone sounded from the console. Takeshi went to check it.

"What is it?"

"A ship is dropping from treb throw," Takeshi informed.

"More fighters?"

"No, a small cargo vessel."

"Any insignias? Who would drive an unarmed ship into an active warzone?"

"No markings of any nobility or corporation. Only the vessel's name: the Progress."

HAILEY SVARTHOLD

A liar's crown. I am the ruler of the Outer Reach. I am a shell of what I once was. I am a Svarthold, like my father, and his father. The empire will never let me rule in my current form. My current form is but a vessel. I am not worthy. I am worthy.

"Dropping from treb throw in 3...2... aaaand here we are," David narrated as the Progress slowed exponentially into the Arcturus system. Everything seemed strangely peaceful; the dim Arcturan star glowing in the distance, Arcturus itself shining like a coin on the ground. Hailey knew that if she could feel butterflies in her chest, now would be the time.

Home. As much as she detested the position she was forced into, she loved Arcturus, and she loved Nymeria. She thought of the cafés and the bright white stone in which they were wrought. She thought of the amphitheatre near the palace grounds and the sounds it broadcast. She thought of the troops that must be trampling through the streets and the fires they were setting in their wake. She thought of Francis and missed him deeply. She thought of her father and missed him, too.

"The Karakura fleet," David mentioned as he pointed to a 3D readout of the system. "Obliterated."

They began to pass a graveyard, the warmth of which had yet to be stolen by the depths of space. Pieces and fragments of once proud ships drifted like ash, silent and foreboding. Karakura pride struck down like they'd received a knife in the back. *Where is the fleet that did this? Why are we unassailed while a noble military lingers in pieces?*

"We still have at least twenty hours until we enter wideband range of Arcturus," David informed. "We should assume there is an opposing military presence somewhere in the system, obviously. If they're in orbit, there will be blind spots that we can take advantage of." He turned the chair and spent a few moments looking at Hailey intently. Clara noticed and silently synchronized. "Hailey," David began, calling for her attention. She broke her gaze from the front window to match David's stare. "Are you sure you want to do this?"

David, dammit, I haven't been sure of anything since I've come back to life. Could you not tell? Hailey pondered the question. *What end am I hoping for? Could I really convince the people of Arcturus to rally under my banner?*

After a short pause, David set free a hopeless sigh just as a notification sounded on the ship's display.

"What is it?" Hailey said, trying her best to sound grounded and confident.

"A... hailing request."

"And?"

"Well, it's from the fleet."

"Ok, which fleet?" Hailey asked, growing timorous. "There are several in this system."

"No, I mean *this fleet.*" David gestured vaguely at the debris outside the window.

"*The Karakura fleet?*" Hailey was nearing her wit's end, and she hadn't yet made planetfall. "Just open the message." David activated the message, and it played.

A window on the screen popped up to show a video. There were two men floating in zero G in a dimly lit escape pod. One spoke: "This is a wideband broadcast to the Progress. This is Takeshi Yamada, Navigation Officer of the Maelstrom of the Karakura Navy, Fifth Fleet. Onboard with me, I have Kenji Karakura, Rear Admiral. We have important information about the nature of the attack on our fleet. We request pick-up and safe transport. Please respond, Progress. I feel we're the only survivors of the attack."

The three stared at the screen blankly. If Hailey had a jaw, it would be on the floor.

"Holy shit," Clara exhaled. "What are the chances?"

"Open a response," Hailey commanded. David began typing on the keyboard in front of him.

"Recording," he informed after a window showing their images appeared on screen.

"This is Hailey Svarthold, rightful Lord of the Outer Reach." The words felt like a foreign language. "Please accept docking permissions and lock to our bulkhead. We will receive you. Progress enroute."

A few minutes later, the breaching pod from the Maelstrom locked and the two boarded. Hailey noticed that they must have been floating for days. Kenji's hair was unkempt, his dress blues messy and wrinkled, but what she noticed most prominently were his eyes. He looked tired, like he had not slept once in his life. The kind of fatigue that was typically associated with high levels of stress, and Hailey could understand why, after everything he'd been through.

Kenji and Hailey stared at each other for a moment with a shared look that asked, '*What happened to you?*

"We have a lot to discuss," Hailey told the two new passengers. "I'm sure you have questions, I have my own. Let's get you guys some food."

Hailey and Kenji had briefly met once, years prior when the Karakura family visited Arcturus to show their respect to Gunnar Svarthold and the Pteron, the legendary battleship he piloted into battle. Hailey remembered that Kenji, and similarly every Karakura, was reserved; a stoicism born from generations of duty and honor. They moved like statues that had just had life breathed into them, still shaking the shale from their joints.

In the modest living quarters of the Progress, Hailey told Kenji what she was, and why she was. Less biological, but no less a Svarthold.

Eventually, after considering much, Kenji asked, "So you still remember that?"

"Which part?"

"Seeing me and my family on Arcturus?"

"I do."

Kenji tilted his head slightly, then nodded pensively. "I should probably tell you what happened to our fleet, and what we're up against."

The mystery that brought her back to Arcturus; Hailey had been waiting patiently for the answer since she first saw the news article on Titan. "We were destroyed by imperial ships."

When David asked if Hailey still wanted to do this, she didn't know how to answer. She was caught like a sheet of paper in a tempest; enveloped by doubt, powerlessly thrown about as the winds decided. Upon hearing about the empire's clandestine involvement in the conflict, she grew excited to see her people once again.

SIMON CANSBY

"Do you have everything you need?" Avery asked Simon as he donned his armor. It was a meditative process that gave him time to reflect on his mission at hand. *A farm boy,* he thought. *How did I go from corn shucker to Imperial Inquisitor?*

"Everything except a ship."

"We've got that covered." Simon met Avery's eyes as he said this, noticing a wry smile crack on the paladin's face. "I think you're gonna like what we have set up for you." Simon's excitement grew and matched his mentor's smile.

"This doesn't seem real."

"I felt the same way when I was knighted. It's daunting, I know, but I could see from early on that you were going to make a phenomenal paladin." Avery stepped closer and put a hand on Simon's shoulder. "We shouldn't speak of pride in the order, but I know you'll make us proud."

"Are you sure? Isn't there a more experienced paladin that can take on this mission?"

"There will always be more experienced people to handle certain tasks, but that isn't the point. You had insight into Harbrand's goings-on during a critical time. You also showed remarkable skill during the investigation into Edgar Thrawl's crimes. The council feels you're best suited for this mission. Besides, it's a basic inquisition. You may be going into a war zone, but they aren't asking you to fight. You have the emperor's blessing, and any noble family would be foolish to step in your way."

With Simon's nerves temporarily placated, he let out a brief sigh and said, "Let's see this ship, then."

Avery accompanied Simon during his walk to the fields of flowers in which the ships sat, a stark dichotomy of intelligent design cast against a background of wild nature. As they approached a landing pad, passing the statues of former paladins flanking the walking path, Simon became surprised, then confused. Avery noticed and said, "He requested you personally. He said he felt the two of you had a great rapport."

Waiting in the gentle rain ahead of them was Bill, standing beneath the looming Persistence.

"There he is!" Bill announced. "*SIR* Simon Cansby. Paladin of the Order," Bill chuckled and threw his arms wide to embrace Simon. "Congratulations, you've earned it."

The words warmed Simon as the two parted. "Thank you, Bill. I'm relieved to have you as my pilot."

Bill clapped his hands together. "Well, enough waiting around. I'll get her warmed up. We leave at your command." He nodded his head to Avery and disappeared into the Persistence.

Avery turned to Simon. "I would start with the Glassers. They're the Lords of the Core and the Harbrands are their bannermen. Establish your authority as Imperial Inquisitor and the doors should open. The admiral of the fleets is Armand Glasser. A tough individual, to be sure, but loyal to the empire. That should make him malleable." Simon nodded with a confidence that belied uncertainty.

"Thank you, Rohan. Until we're called upon."

"Until we're called upon, *Sir* Simon Cansby."

Upon the ship, Simon attempted to settle in. Though he had spent weeks aboard this vessel, it all felt brand new to him. Bill entered the cockpit and sat in his chair.

"Isn't this just exciting?" he said in a giddy tone.

"It's something." Excitement was just scratching the surface for Simon.

"I know where we're going, should be dangerous," Bill chuckled. "I wait for your command."

Simon thought for a moment, then confided, "Bill, we have a secondary objective. One that the council doesn't know about, so this requires your discretion."

Bill turned, smiled, and nodded. "I trust you, Simon. Even if we break a couple of rules, I know you're doing it for the right reason." *Sometimes you have to break with tradition to make progress.* "So, what's this secret mission?"

"Harbrand let his pride and hubris blind him to the intentions of Henry Svarthold. I recently learned that Hailey Svarthold, his daughter, committed suicide shortly before Henry became a fugitive. I don't believe that a man like Henry would create a resurrective technology only to revive a criminal to get revenge on the Harbrands. That was Henry's attempt at obfuscation, and it worked, but there is another that he revived. I believe Hailey Svarthold is still alive and we'll find her on Arcturus."

DAMIR BLACKHAT

How, out of all people, did someone like Henry Svarthold figure it out? Damir rubbed his eyes as he sat for the thirteenth consecutive hour at his computer reviewing data, with a headless autonomous android lying lifeless on the countertop behind him, covered in dust. *How did he quantify consciousness?*

The door to his laboratory slid open and Commandant Keeran Wulfstadt entered. Keeran was a tall, thin man, with black, beady eyes set in contrast to his alabaster skin. He wore a ceramic nano-weave chest plate beneath a white lab coat to show his dual roles: warrior and scientist. He was the primary combat theoretician of the ruling families of the Core and was famous for his ruthless inventions and merciless experiments. Damir stood at attention.

"What have you found?" Keeran asked in a controlled, almost hushed tone.

"Commandant, I have poured over this drone, but without the engram in its head, I haven't been able to figure out how any of it worked." Damir's hands shook as he held them behind his back.

"I have figured as much. You must understand that this is a disappointment, yes?"

"Yes, sir, Commandant."

"Good. Now, if we were able to retrieve a working engram, you would be able to replicate its secrets, correct? Could you guarantee me this?"

Damir knew to choose his next words carefully. To deny Wulfstadt was worse than failing him, but Damir could still easily fail in replicating the Consciousness Matrix Engram even with a working one. "My lord, I thought he only made the one, which was destroyed in the Barcelona system."

"We have word from our contact that there is another." Keeran turned to look out the window. Beyond the glass was the arcing horizon of Arcturus. "And it may be on its way here now. Can you guarantee me your success?" The tone of Wulfstadt's voice seemed to pull color out of the air.

"Yes, my lord." Damir knew he had sealed his fate, but he had no choice.

"Fantastic." Keeran turned and met Damir's eyes with a smile that betrayed his attempts at trying to look more human, a clear facsimile of empathy. "Now, in the meantime we may need your... other invention."

Damir's eyes widened in surprise, then in alarm. "My lord, if the emperor finds out what I've made, he could burn down every throneworld in the core. It's a blatant violation of imperial law, and we would be beset upon by the order and its paladins."

"I understand, but we need your invention's discretion to hunt down this engram. Besides, after what the emperor did to the Karakura fleet, we have a little leverage. What we're doing here is for the emperor, after all. How we meet those ends, well, he doesn't need to be any the wiser." Keeran now cracked a sinister smile that more accurately reflected his heart. "Awaken the Rakshasa."

KENJI KARAKURA

Kenji woke. The simple act took him by surprise as he hadn't had a peaceful night's sleep for as long as he could remember. Refreshed, he lifted himself to sitting position in the modest cabin bunk aboard the Progress.

Comfortable? The thought flashed in his mind, a picture of his mother tucking him into bed, asking him the same question. Kenji looked around, attempting to find the source. It seemed simultaneously stolen and given back.

He saw Hopper in the doorway peering at him.

"Was that you?" Kenji asked, stifling his alarm. He had seen the little entity when he arrived on the Progress, but Hopper had kept his distance from the two new guests until now.

Yes, an image of his father answering a simple question. *I apologize,* a servant of the Karakura family atoning for his mistakes. *I hope this isn't too intrusive,* Kenji's mother expressing empathy for cramped quarters during a long trip. *It's how I communicate.*

"I uh... yes, I'm comfortable." *Can you read my thoughts?*

Yes. The response startled Kenji, his wide eyes betrayed the stillness he was projecting. *Please don't worry, though.* Hopper stepped beyond the threshold of Kenji's room. *Most minds are too tumultuous to read, too much going on, so I can only sense what's at the front of one's thoughts. You can read mine, too. I project my thoughts, even when I don't mean to.*

Kenji allowed for a moment of reprise and gathered himself, still sitting bedside. "So, why are you here?"

Adventure. I have been a friend of David's for some time, so when the chance came, we both set forth.

"You have no duty to your people?"

This, duty, is a concept my people are not familiar with. We believe each of us is not beholden to the many. Most of our ambitions are humble and singular, and we typically do not plan for the future. Kenji thought about the liberation a lack of duty would give him. He imagined himself studying anomalies on the edge of the galaxy, enveloping his mind in the greater mysteries of the cosmos. *I see you don't much like it, but duty can give purpose to one that would otherwise be bereft of it. You may see it that way, eventually, rather than a burden.*

I don't think I will. I'm a coward that abandoned his post. I may not have duty for very long. I may not feel needed soon.

You're needed here.

Clara Brightwater knocked on the doorframe and poked her head in. "Hey," she said in a pillowy tone, paired with a soft smile and empathetic eyes. Kenji felt his heart flutter for a moment. "I didn't want to wake you earlier. How are you holding up?"

"Great!" Kenji stammered. "Well, I mean about as great as I can be, given, well... the whole thing. The whole like, uh. You get it."

Clara smirked. Hopper projected the thought of a warm, percipient smile to Kenji and quietly left the room.

Clara approached and sat next to Kenji on his bunk. A sudden worry, forgotten for the first time in years, returned to his mind. It had been days, maybe weeks, since Kenji had bathed. *Do I smell?* He shifted nervously.

Kenji stole looks at Clara as she stared into the middle distance, gathering her thoughts next to him. Dark brown hair tied back in a loose knot, deep blue eyes cast upon pale skin. Kenji thought she looked like a visage of sorrow, solemn and beautiful, like a marble statue carved with its arms held out beckoning for an embrace. Clara turned her head and met Kenji's gaze. He was captured; Kenji had left one Maelstrom only to be caught by another.

Clara looked as though she were about to ask one question, then switched to a different one. "How are you feeling? What you've been through, it's so much."

"Well," he began after sighing, "my father and I were never close, I was always closer with my mother. Still, it feels strange. I know I should be sad, but I'm just... hollow." Clara watched Kenji with apathetic eyes and remained silent. "My life is also forfeit; I hold no titles because I abandoned my post. It was either that or die. I guess I'm just lost."

"I've forfeited my titles, too. I just hope that eventually, history can reflect what I've done, and my family will understand."

"I don't think I'll even get that. According to Karakura traditions, one should die in battle. I'm considered a traitor."

Clara recoiled slightly at the word. The two spent a moment in reflective silence. "Do you... do you think any of this is worth it?" Clara asked, her voice shaking slightly.

Kenji finally picked up that something was bothering Clara. He wondered why she was confiding in him and not one of the crewmates that knew her better. "What do you mean?"

"All this… struggle," Clara said, flustered. "We have so many ties to family and duty. So many responsibilities, rules, expectations. My family's legacy is more important than my own life, my own choices. Is it worth it? Nobility?"

"Honestly, I don't know," Kenji responded. "I've spent my entire life wishing that I could be just a common person, no noble name or lineage. Just drifting through the cosmos with nothing tying me down. But after I saw my legacy obliterated, floating out there, I've been feeling guilty. There are some things I'll miss about my home and my people. Things, otherwise unnoticed, that seem to manifest only in hindsight." This didn't seem to make Clara feel any better. "I'm happy to be making new friends, though. You and your crew have been wonderful to me."

With this, Clara's eyes began welling with tears. She gave Kenji a look that seemed like she could be shattered like glass; the marble cracking, still waiting for the embrace. She left the room in a hurry. Kenji sat, speechless.

He gathered his thoughts and left the bunk room a short while later. He fixed his hair and put on some extra clothes that the crew had in storage aboard the Progress.

He gathered with almost everyone in the cockpit: David, Takeshi, Hopper, and Hailey. Clara wasn't present. After her reaction to what Kenji said, it seemed like she needed time alone.

Hailey stood, arms crossed, staring out the front window. She had on brown robes over her android form, the desert veil pulled back to reveal a featureless, brushed steel face. The image of the last Svarthold was a strange thing for Kenji to behold, the will of a god created by the hand of man. Whether out of hubris, pure love, or heedless action, Henry had turned his daughter into a statement - a clear defiance of nature, imperial law and the wishes of others. Resurrection was a powerful symbol. *How will the emperor feel about this? She's riding such a dangerously fine line with what imperial law declares illegal. Am I duty bound to stop her, or help her?*

As though Hailey could hear his thoughts, she turned and caught Kenji looking at her. "I know," she admitted.

"What?"

"Seeing me like this, it's weird. I would rather have stayed dead, honestly."

Kenji wasn't sure how to respond. Weird was only the beginning, her entire existence was contradictory. "So, why keep going?"

"If I'm going to be forced to be alive, I may as well do something good. My father abandoned his people, I need to pick up where he left off."

Kenji realized that even without a biological form, Hailey had something he did not: purpose. Kenji felt like one of the fragments of his family's fleet.

"Wideband range," David informed. "The fleets will be on the other side of the planet for a couple of hours. It would be smart to break atmosphere away from Nymeria and travel there by land. It's now or never."

Hailey nodded, "Take us in."

SIMON CANSBY

"Why did nobody tell me about this?" Simon asked, stunned, staring at the Karakura graveyard floating in space in front of the Persistence. The destruction was absolute and terrifying to look at. *Corn shucker to Imperial Inquisitor. Why am I here?* "How long until we're in wideband range?"

"About seventeen hours, I can get this thing going pretty damn fast," Bill replied with a smirk.

"Good, get us there. I need to have a chat with Armand Glasser."

The Persistence set forth.

Bill and Simon waited during transit. Neither slept, Simon paced, Bill tried to listen to music, but decided he wasn't in the mood for it. Seventeen hours advanced at a crawl. The inevitable gloom of a warzone slowly grew in the windows of the Persistence.

"Alright, we're in wideband range," Bill announced as Simon stood a few feet away, deep in thought.

Snapping out of his trance, Simon looked onward out the window to Arcturus. Looming silently above were the fleets of the Core. They looked small from this distance, but Simon knew the might they had hidden away. "Open up a hailing channel."

"Done."

"This is Sir Simon Cansby, Paladin of the Order of the Lesser, requesting audience with Armand Glasser. I am an inquisitor sent by the Council of Scholars, with the blessing of Emperor Desmond VII."

The recording ended. "Now we wait," Bill said, allowing silence to fill the air.

Five minutes later, a notification popped up on the readout. Bill tapped it and started the playback.

"This is Armand Glasser of the Peregrin, Grand Admiral of the Glasser Fleet." Armand stood among a well-lit bridge, surrounded by terminals manned by officers dressed in dark grey uniforms. Armand had black, swept back hair down to his shoulders, dark eyes, and a short, well-kept beard. "You will be welcome aboard our ship and among the Glassers, Sir Cansby. You are cleared to land in Bay 4, I will personally receive you. We'll see you soon."

Playback ended. Simon took a deep breath and said, "Take us in." Bill nodded and the Persistence resumed travel.

The fleets of the Core hovered motionless above an awaiting Arcturus. Simon thought it looked like they were flying into a portrait. As they neared, the Peregrin grew impossibly large, as though it were expanding to intimidate the Persistence. A vessel shot out from one of the bays in the ship and flew away from the fleets, towards Nymeria.

Simon noticed two other fleets, flying in a triangle formation with the Glassers. He knew one was the Harbrand fleet, and the other belonged to the Blackhats. The power of the combined fleet had the potential to conquer the expanse of the empire.

The Persistence approached Bay 4. Bulkheads the size of cargo vessels began to separate from one another, revealing an open landing bay in the port side of the freighter. A silver sheen appeared between them as the gap grew; the gravity field holding the atmosphere in while the doors were open.

Bill guided the Persistence into the bay and down onto a landing pad. Around them were fighters designed for quick flight and swift strikes, vicious and efficient. Simon noticed something that all the ships in all three fleets had in common.

"Bill," he said as the Persistence touched down, "all these ships are spotless. They're brand new. Like they've never seen battle."

DAMIR BLACKHAT

What have I done? Damir watched as the small courier vessel began to shrink as it neared Arcturus. *What have I done?* An invention that granted his life permit to continue. The brutal Blackhat warrior culture had little need for scientists. *What have I done?* Damir felt as though he were the only one among his people to feel empathy.

What have I done?

Before Damir had left for Arcturus, before he had started his career as a military scientist, before he was allowed to keep living, he breathed life into an invention that would undo him.

Intellectuals on the Blackhat throneworld, Crenelation, were considered a luxury. Tradesmen and soldiers were all that were needed in a culture that began as a private military company under the employ of the Glassers during the Conquest. Damir had never been a fighter but needed to prove his worth before he was culled.

Rakshasa, he had named it, to express the sinister nature of its existence. After activating it for the first time, he shut down the Rakshasa and wept. Later, Damir installed a master kill switch that could be triggered by him at any moment.

He had never told anyone about the master kill switch.

"Brilliant timing," Keeran Wulfstadt whispered, arms behind his back. "The Rakshasa ship passed right under the paladin's nose. He shouldn't be any the wiser."

Damir felt like he was made of sand, as though a gentle breeze could scatter him. "Sir, if I may." It took every bit of strength in him to keep his voice from shaking violently. "I don't know if we should move forward with this. A paladin shows up within hours of us activating the... Rakshasa? That can't be coincidence. It's an AI drone, if he finds out, the entire siege could be undone. I think we should recall—"

"*Enough,*" Keeran hissed in response. He approached Damir with intimidating swiftness, stopping inches from his face. "I will not have my orders questioned by you. Another word spoken in doubt, and I will personally see that you're breathing vacuum in—" Keeran stopped himself, took a breath, shook off his lab coat and continued, "Faith, Damir. Faith in your cause, in your family, in your legacy."

"Yes, my lord."

HAILEY SVARTHOLD

"Horses?" Hailey asked no one in particular. "We're taking horses?"

"Quadruped Robotic Drones, or QRDs, to be precise," David responded without looking up from his maintenance of one of the vehicles. "Robust, quiet. These things can get over rough terrain better than anything with wheels."

Before them stood five robotic drones in the general shape of horses. Painted a construction yellow, with exposed wires and motors hastily zip-tied in place. None had heads in the traditional sense, but rather a form of handlebars, at the center of which was a simple readout for travel data.

David procured these vehicles at a farming equipment retailer and repair shop in the small town where they landed. Though he liked to use the technical name for these inventions, Hailey noticed that the locals simply called them horses.

"Rough terrain? We couldn't use anything with anti-grav in it?" Clara inquired.

"The mercury drives that we use to create a zero-g field are, ironically, too large. We wouldn't be able to keep our presence hidden while moving toward Nymeria, as the sieging armies have ways to track mercury drive use." He moved closer to one of the horses. "These things, however," he gave one an affectionate slap, "these are old-school, analog. No way to track 'em other than line of sight."

"Made all the more clandestine by their paintjob," Hailey retorted. She could hear Clara snicker behind her. "Once we're there, how do we get in without being noticed?"

"I'm not sure." David turned away from the horses. "But we have a few days ride until we're there. We'll approach from the south and scout the area. Nymeria's a big city, so I'm sure we'll find a point of entry."

A few days ride, Hailey thought. The words sounded ridiculous, like they were plucked out of a medieval novel. The juxtaposition of the intimidating length of time against the absurd nature of the statement in a time where humans travelled distances a billion times farther in a fraction of the time made everything seem more surreal than it already was.

"Well..." Hailey looked to her party, her island of misfit toys, and saw them awaiting her command. *Svarthold, daughter of my father.* "Mount up."

Hailey was familiar with the classics of literature and knew that some of them went as far back to a time when people rode horses as a primary means of transportation. Enigmatic nomads and headstrong heroes flung to the edges of their known world, the horizon an immutable barrier that never barred any entry, but only continued to back away, beckoning the hero to follow. She noticed now that her journey may not be so glamorous, as she wasn't all that far from where she was born.

Each of the members of her party had a *horse*, except for Hopper, who rode with David. During passage, Hopper occasionally stood and looked around, silently shouting, calling out to the plant life around him. The others would turn their head and react, oohs and aahs as flowers would bloom, or stalks of what seemed like knee-high grass would recede down to a few inches in height, all at the word of this little master. Kenji and Takeshi would laugh and point, David would respond to silent jokes and Clara would smile.

Hailey rode on, deaf to Hopper's words and unable to participate, like she was watching them through a window.

After a few hours, David commanded his horse up to where Hailey was at the front of the party. "How does it feel? Being home?" Hailey turned her featureless face to see David change his expression at the sight. With her being nigh unreadable, David looked like he wasn't sure if he offended Hailey and started to back pedal nervously. "Uh, Hopper was curious." Hopper snapped a look at David; Hailey assumed they were communicating – arguing – about the context of the question.

Hailey looked back to the path and let out a small chuckle. "I feel ok. It's a mixed bag, really. A lot of who I am is here, but a lot of who I didn't want to be is here as well."

Pensive, David looked on in silence, bobbing slightly from the gait of the horse.

"You know I haven't commanded any of you to remain, right?" Hailey inserted. "Not that I'm ungrateful for everything you and Clara have done, aside from raising me from the dead." From the way David's shoulders slumped almost imperceptibly, Hailey knew he felt at least a little guilty. "But I'm not trying to hold my sovereignty over your head. Why are you sticking with this? With me?"

David paused briefly, then answered, "Your father saved my sister's life." Hailey faced him silently, an invitation to elaborate. "A long time ago, she had a degenerative neural disorder. My parents spent every resource our family had; every favor called in. Even the best doctors from the Imperial Hospital on Titan couldn't figure it out. My parents were desperate, so they put out an open plea to anyone that could help. With his background in neuroscience, Henry stepped in." Hailey listened attentively, never knowing this part of her father's history. "After a few weeks of research and another of treatment, she began to recover. She's married to the Lord of Sinisi now, and I have little nieces and nephews running around because of what Henry did." David began to smile as his eyes got misty. "My father swore a new allegiance to Henry after that. A thousand years of loyalty to the Svarthold name is what he promised.

"I read it in the reports, I know my father rescinded troops and fleets from defending Arcturus. What you don't know is that when I told my father that I was going to help Henry bring his daughter back, and that it would look terrible for our family, he told me, '*A Hill knows where his honor lies.*' His duty, and mine, wasn't to Arcturus or the Outer Reach, it was to your father, carried from my father to me, from your father to you. When the time comes, I know you can call on the Hills and they will respond in kind."

Hailey, taken aback, wasn't sure how to respond. She craned her head to look at the rest of her followers. The Karakuras pledged their allegiance to Gunnar Svarthold, the Hills to Henry. Hailey felt a sudden weight of regret as she realized she didn't know enough about the good things her family had done over the generations. *Svarthold.*

SIMON CANSBY

They crippled an entire planet, Simon stewed, *and an additional fleet, and not so much as a scratch.*

He sat in the loading bay on the underside of the Persistence, the ramp opened at an angle to meet the floor of the ship bay aboard the Peregrin. Perched on top of a storage container, he examined the Glasser crew as they went about their business: stocking, loading, inspecting, cleaning.

Hanging from the ceiling of the bay were rows of small fighter ships, named Kestrels, Simon learned. Painted matte black, the harsh angles of the Kestrels projected an intimidating visage. They hung with their noses to the floor, wings folded, like neat rows of bats.

Not one was out of place. None of them were missing or being repaired or restocked.

The Persistence boarded the Peregrin a day prior. Simon was met with warm hospitality from the Lord of the Core, Armand Glasser.

As Simon descended the loading bay ramp, glaive in hand, he was received by Armand and his lessers. One was pale, dressed in black beneath black armor, the other was seven feet tall. Clearly the Lords Blackhat and Harbrand, respectively.

"It is humbling to have a Paladin of the Order of the Lesser aboard our ship, Sir Cansby," Armand announced in an assertive, but not hostile, tone. *Perfectly befitting a man of his command,* Simon noted. *So perfect, it seemed rehearsed.* Armand saluted in Glasser fashion, with his right fist pressed against his heart, followed by a curt bow. The men flanking him repeated the gesture. "I am Armand Glasser, Lord of the Core. This is Petrev Blackhat, Lord of Crenelation," he said motioning to the man in black, "and this is Nathaniel Harbrand, Lord of Hoard." Armand turned and motioned to the seven-foot-tall man dressed in grey and red military regalia, who nodded his head toward Simon. Hidden within his stony expression was the slightest hint of contempt. *So, he knows who I am, then.*

"My lords," Simon reciprocated a respectful response, bowing curtly, "thank you for receiving me, it is an honor." While facing the floor, Simon caught his banner hanging from below the blade of his glaive out of the corner of his eye. The Cansby Mill, sand on navy blue; a familiar sight seen in a new light, the banner brand new, not yet blemished from use.

"Very well, let us retire to the war room. As Inquisitor, I assume you have questions." Armand turned and made space between himself and Lord Harbrand - a clear sign that Simon should fall in line and follow the Lords.

Simon's mind raced as he marched through the hallways of the Peregrin, flanked by some of the most powerful men in the galaxy. *What do you think you'll be able to ask them, corn shucker?* Simon asked himself, frustration welling as he spiraled.

He thought about Boe *'Come back to me'* and he thought about Damion. Simon recalled the day he buried his brother beneath the mill, the day his life changed irrevocably. Simon would love to give it up and embrace Boe and live out his remaining years with her. He thought about burying his glaive and shield next to his brother, but knew that if he did, it would be little different than if he lay in that grave himself.

Imperial Inquisitor. He stored away the memory of Boe's smile, her laugh, her vibrant blue eyes. Simon gathered the memories of her like he was straightening a messy bedroom, each thought a scrap of paper caught in the wind of an open window. Each memory a pile of clothes, an unmade bed, a film of dust. Simon cleaned this room until it looked like no one had ever set foot inside.

The war room was set up in a circle, an elevated platform in the middle of a room of stations, readouts shining brightly from the table amid the platform. The room was painted a clinical grey, matching the uniforms of the soldiers that sat at each station.

As they approached, Simon could see some of the information being projected above the war-room table. Numbers, trajectories, readouts, it was all a jumble to Simon with no context, apart from the occasional news article that would pop up briefly.

Journalists were hard at work on the frontlines of Arcturus, during one of the most important events in the galaxy's recent memory. '*Nymerian Landmark Crumbles from Bombing.*' The titles of the articles sprawled across the screen before disappearing. '*Resident Refuses to Relocate Amidst Siege,*' '*Second Victim of Beheading Found,*' '*Emperor Remains Silent as Claims of War Crimes Go Unanswered.*'

The feed disappeared altogether, snapping Simon's attention back to the eyes of the Lords around the table, all on him.

"So, Sir Cansby," Armand started, "as we understand it, an inquisitor from the Paladins is uncommon. I've made several attempts at guessing why the Council has sent you here, but I'm afraid I haven't come up with an answer." It was clear to Simon that that statement was a prompt for him to fill in the gaps, to finally begin his inquisition. He took a deep breath.

DAMIR BLACKHAT

Damir was only a child when he saw his sister taken in the night. It was the final attempt by their parents to awaken a warrior within her. Tossed into the wilderness, she was commanded to survive.

Damir's parents returned that evening without her and informed him of what had taken place. If she didn't return, then she had been culled, and the family would be better for it.

Damir sat by the window for days, he didn't sleep or eat, he just waited, stirring at the slightest movement of the trees beyond the wall of his family's compound.

He waited for three days.

He waited four. Then five. The hope of his sister's return was like a small campfire struggling to stay alight.

On the sixth day, Damir broke, and the fire was snuffed out.

I think it may be worth it, Damir thought. He had been staring out of the window at Arcturus for over an hour, unmoving. *I can either die out there, having done the right thing, or live, knowing what I've done, among a family I loathe.* Damir's shoulders relaxed for the first time since he was a child; the relief from his jaw unclenching made it feel as though it were about to fall off.

Keeran Wulfstadt entered the room, robotic in his steps. "Why is this happening?" He showed an article to Damir from his tablet.

"Sir, I believe it's because it is looking for the engram." Damir's calm demeanor was plain enough that Keeran paused to investigate him briefly. "Since the engram is located in the head, it makes sense that it's interpreting the programming literally."

Keeran responded with a long, suspicious stare, then commanded, "Fix it."

"Yes sir, Commandant." Damir suppressed a smile as he thought about just how he would fix it.

KENJI KARAKURA

"And then he..." Takeshi had to stop himself, laughter encroached as he regaled the group with a story about him and Kenji when they were young. Regaining his composure, he continued, "I swear on my life, he just turns and slaps the kid square in the face." Kenji and Takeshi burst out into raucous laughter reciprocated with only confused stares from the rest of the group, their smiles hanging as though they were still waiting to hear a punchline.

I guess you had to be there, a thought projected by Hopper. From the way that everyone else began laughing, Kenji surmised that he projected it to the group.

Takeshi, embarrassed, but still smiling, raised his hands in a conceding motion. "Look, I might not be the best storyteller, but his face was priceless."

The group sat around a campfire, telling stories in the dim glow. Kenji had felt a sense of trepidation throughout the day, the dread of the warzone looming ever closer as they approached. The feeling around the campfire was different, he noted. It was as if the flames set them on an island of light among a sea of night. Like they were outside time, if only for a little while. The mood was airy and fun, for the first time since Kenji was young.

"I went to a private school," Clara spoke, her voice almost smoky as she sat next to Kenji. "One that the ruling class families of the Outer Reach sent all their kids to. We—"

"The Cidrius Academy?" Hailey interjected.

Clara smirked. "Yes, that one."

"*Yikes,*" Hailey replied, snickering after a short pause.

Clara's eyebrows furled, still smirking. "Bite me."

"I'm joking." Hailey elongated the word while raising her hands. Kenji knew, impossibly, that Hailey was smiling. "Please continue."

"So, when I was in school, for some reason Margaret Kopesh hated me."

"The Kopeshes suck so much," Takeshi chimed in.

"I know," Clara rolled her eyes. "She convinced everyone that I was... *promiscuous.* I had boys constantly giving me gross advances, feeling like it was a sure thing. I *hated* it. Anything I tried to say to counteract her lies was just brushed off; '*Yeah, sure,*' '*You're just projecting,*' things like that.

"At one point, as a boy came over to try and convince me to sleep with him, I could see Margaret watching us. Normally, she would watch with a jagged grin plastered on her face, incredibly proud of what she'd done. This time, she looked concerned, apprehension in her eyes. I realized that she liked this boy."

Hailey was leaning forward, completely engrossed. Kenji was as well, but for different reasons. Clara's eyes seemed to glow purple, the red of the fire mingling with the already present icy blue. The flames cast dramatic shadows that accentuated every movement her face made as she told her anecdote. Kenji was grateful Clara had decided to share, he used this as an excuse to stare at her unapologetically, to soak up every detail.

Clara continued, "Lean into it, I thought. Consequences of her own actions and all that. So, I pretended to like the boy back. I laughed at his jokes, played with my hair, gave him suggestive looks. After a minute or two of pretending, I reached out and grabbed his hand. I looked over at Margaret and her face was, as Takeshi put it, priceless. I winked at her, and she cried and ran out of there as fast as possible."

"That's vicious," Hailey commented with a tone of admiration. "I met Margaret Kopesh once and she was terrible to be around. Good work."

"What happened next? Like with the boy?" David clarified after an inquisitive look from Clara.

"Oh! Yeah, I just told him I changed my mind like five minutes later." They laughed. Clara justified, "Look, I'm not proud of it. I try to take the high road when I can, but I had to sink to her level to eke out a victory. And it had been *months* of pestering from the boys. I was sick of it."

Clara caught Kenji looking at her. She held his gaze for a moment, before Kenji panicked and looked away in a hurry. Kenji shifted, then Clara put her head on his shoulder.

Kenji realized something then: he couldn't remember the last time anyone had touched him.

Gentle contact like this was so alien to him and it felt like a drug. He became lightheaded, he felt his heartbeat in his ears, rapid and percussive. He became mindful of every breath to keep from breathing too loud.

Everyone turned pensive as they stared into the flames, a warm kind of quiet, accented with occasional cracks and pops from the fire that entranced them, becoming thralls to its hypnotic dance.

"Woah, damn," David exclaimed, looking up from his tablet. "There's some kind of serial killer or something loose in Nymeria. This article says they're beheading women. It started a couple of days ago."

"Does it say why?" Hailey asked. "Anything as to motives? Or is it just killing for the sake of killing?"

"Doesn't look like they have a lot of information, but I think a person who's cutting people's heads off won't likely have justifiable motives."

A heavy silence fell over the group; the light of the fire seemingly dimming in front of them.

SIMON CANSBY

"We need to know how you were informed." Simon apprised the lords. "The Council of Scholars needs to know where you got your information about the death of Henry Svarthold."

Armand Glasser gave a slight, solemn nod. "Ah, I see."

"Is it any wonder they sent you, Sir Cansby?" Nathaniel Harbrand counter-interrogated. "From what I understand, you were Acolyte under Alan Harbrand's instruction." His voice was venomous. It was clear to Simon that he felt this was an affront to his family's name. Simon couldn't say what his face was doing at that moment, but he hoped it didn't show fear, though he felt it immensely.

"Lord Harbrand, I can understand your feelings on the matter," Glasser interjected, "but we cannot be harassing an imperial agent, no matter our feelings." Harbrand let out a huff; he seemed to be backing down, though he continued to watch Simon intensely. "Now, Simon, if I may call you that, you must understand that we have agents and informants all over the galaxy. We didn't need Sir Alan Harbrand's involvement to ascertain that knowledge." Simon could feel it: the set up to a lie. Glasser had been too genial since he had arrived on the Peregrin. Some of what he was saying may be the truth, but Simon was certain not all of it was. He continued to watch and listen.

Glasser carried on, "I cannot go into finer detail about my networks of informants, you understand, but I can tell you this for a certainty: Sir Alan Harbrand did not inform us about the death of Henry Svarthold." They had successfully backed Simon into a corner before he could even begin his inquisition. Clear denial of Alan's involvement, with an unverifiable excuse for how the information was attained. Simon couldn't think, every thought blurred in his mind as a wordless amalgamation. He stood quietly in front of them for too long a moment.

"I regret that you have come all this way for that, Cansby," Harbrand broke the silence, "but if there's nothing else, we would like to get back to our work here." He began to walk away.

Simon had an epiphany and his eyes lit up. *Challenge him.*

"My title is *Sir* Cansby, as befits a *Paladin* of the Order. I'm sure you're familiar, Lord Harbrand. Your nephew, Sir Alan Harbrand, has been a paladin for a very long time. I request that you respectfully refer to me by the same title." Harbrand turned back slowly. Simon met his eyes and saw pure rage burning within them, but he stood silent, attentive. "This inquisition is not finished, my lords." Simon's nerves had broken, gone past the point of a fire in his chest, an increase in heartrate, light-headedness. Anxiety had been burned out like a fever. Simon was met with silent attention from the Lords of the Core.

He continued, "At no point did I mention the involvement of Sir Alan Harbrand. Parallel to that, moments ago, Lord Glasser, you told me that you couldn't guess why an inquisition was necessary. After confirming that I came seeking an understanding of how you acquired your information, both you and Lord Harbrand were all too quick to state Sir Alan's defense. I'm sure you *understand* my curiosity," Simon mimicked

Glasser's intonation of the word. "I am an imperial agent," Simon tapped his finger on the table in punctuation, "and I would ask that you not insult my intelligence with such obvious lies. This is not behavior befitting a lord."

Harbrand was as red as his fatigues, and because Simon stared back in defiance, he didn't notice Petrev Blackhat lunge at him, a knife at his throat.

Simon was watching himself, disassociated with the unfamiliar man that stood resistant in front of these powerful lords unshaken, unflinching, unbroken. Without moving his head, his eyes met Lord Blackhat's.

"I should kill you here, you fucking worm," Blackhat hissed. "The Lords of the Core will not be insulted by someone so—"

"PETREV, ENOUGH!" Glasser bellowed, a tone in his voice that Simon hadn't heard previously. "Release the paladin, *now.*" Simon understood then that this was his real voice. The voice of command that intimidated so many; a voice that he had intentionally hidden.

Blackhat released Simon and slithered back to Glasser's side. Glasser's palms set rigidly against the table. "I apologize, Sir Cansby. Please understand that this is not how we typically conduct ourselves." Explaining through gritted teeth, Glasser struggled to excuse his companion. His muscles were tense. He wasn't looking Simon in the eye. The façade was beginning to crack.

Simon straightened himself, allowing a moment to pretend he was disturbed, and was only just regaining composure. "My lords, I'm disappointed," Simon responded. "An Imperial Inquisition is rare, I admit, but I did not expect such resistance. It's plain to me that there are secrets that the three of you would not like seeing the light of day, by means of violence, if necessary." He motioned to Lord Blackhat who returned an icy stare. "You've stated how you'd come to receiving the information of Lord Svarthold's death. Is this the truth?"

Lords Glasser and Harbrand were seething; the former gripping the table in front of him, staring at the ground, the latter red-faced, with clenched fists.

" *Yes,"* Glasser said quietly. Simon backed himself into that same corner. *Keep pushing.*

"Very well," Simon relented. "I would've taken this at face value, but it seems I need to acquire a subpoena from the Council of Scholars in order to obtain the information about your informants," Simon turned his attention to Lord Harbrand, "in order to exonerate Sir Alan, as you must know. He's currently being detained for this suspected conspiracy. I only tell you this out of *transparency,"* Simon emphasized the word. "My lords." He gave a curt bow and began to leave. "My pilot and I will need to stay for a time to rest," Simon informed as he turned mid-departure. "You understand."

So now he sat, ruminating about the meeting, the unscathed ships in the fleets, the implications of his own theories. Perched upon a crate in the underbelly loading bay of the Persistence, he watched the crew go about their business. Simon knew he would have to return to the Council with not enough information, but it would have to do.

"Excuse me." A young man at the bottom of the ramp startled Simon. "You're the paladin, right?"

Simon nodded, a puzzled look on his face. The young man looked around and stepped up the ramp, moving closer to whisper.

"If you take me with you, promise me safe passage, I'll tell you everything you need to know about what's going on here."

"How do you have that information?" Simon whispered back.

"I'm a military scientist and combat theoretician for this siege. My name is Damir Blackhat."

DAMIR BLACKHAT

"Private Contractor," Bill told Damir after he had been staring. "That's why I don't look the government type." Surrounded only by morbidly intense members of military his entire life, Damir was in awe at a man that could look so carefree. *He just lets his facial hair grow like that? The dirty hat, relaxed posture, informal speech; he's allowed to live like this.* "Name's Bill," he informed awkwardly, eyes darting in uncertainty.

"Get us underway, Bill." Simon entered the room. "Make it look like we're in no hurry. Follow their protocol and make a nice, easy exit."

"You got it," Bill confirmed as he turned in his chair. "This is the Corsair Persistence requesting departure from the Peregrin, how copy?" Bill began his routine for take-off.

Simon turned to Damir. "We'll get you out of the system and on the way to Harbor. The Council of Scholars will want all your information."

"I thank you for this."

"No need, it's mutual," Simon smiled warmly.

"But there is something else..." Damir began. Simon's smile started to dwindle. "I can go into more detail about the conspiracy going on here, but there is something you need to fix before we leave the system."

"*I* need to fix?"

"A paladin needs to fix. Quickly."

Simon shook his head in frustration. "What, exactly?"

"I've created a... a demon."

"A demon? What is that supposed to mean? I'll need more information, regarding both your problem and the overall plot going on here. I feel that's only fair."

"The Karakura fleet was destroyed by imperial ships."

Simon's expression remained the same for a moment, then his eyes widened. He looked to Bill slowly, who rotated in his chair equally slowly to meet Simon's stare, eyes just as wide. "Roger, Peregrin, spooling up now," Bill announced over the microphone, his face unchanging.

Damir watched as Simon's entire body language changed. Somehow relaxing and clenching muscles in response, as he put all the pieces together. Simon stared into the middle distance, and let out a brief, exasperated chuckle.

"Please, I'll give you all the details; everything you want to know, confessed to whomever you deem appropriate, but we need to focus on the problem that's down there on Arcturus."

"What is it?" Simon looked up from the floor. "What could possibly be more important than what you're telling me now?"

"I created a super soldier. It's down there hunting, killing ruthlessly."

"Created?"

"An AI drone."

Simon doubled over, crouching with his head in his hands. After a moment, he exploded. "FUCK!" he screamed as he threw his glaive sideways against the wall. It clanged and bounced to the floor. Simon began pacing. "I told them there were more qualified paladins for this mission," he vented to Bill, who paid little attention as he focused on getting Persistence out of, and away from the Peregrin.

"It's hunting someone specific, someone of importance to the war."

"I'm going to take a wild guess and say it's Hailey Svarthold." Simon's voice was poisonous.

Damir recoiled in surprise. "How did you know that?"

"I had my theories. How did you find out she was alive?"

"I don't know exactly who, but Blackhat intelligence has an inside informant. Someone close to her."

Simon thought for a moment, then bowed his head. "Damnit," he said under his breath. "That's how they found out about Henry's death."

The ship beneath them gently separated from the gravity field of the colossal command ship.

Damir looked to the front windows and almost started to weep as he saw it. Open space; the first step away from the oppression of his family.

"I can tell you with certainty that I don't want to stay in this system any more than you do," Damir asserted, "but there is a problem out there that both of us need to eliminate. I am responsible and must see this through, and you swore an oath." Simon and Damir's eyes bore into each other with uniform intensity, and silence stole the room. "By this, we are duty-bound."

HAILEY SVARTHOLD

The truth will be enough. These people, your people, need leadership and they've been left deprived of it. Tell them, convince them, that this body is just a shell. Svarthold, daughter of my father.

Hailey rocked gently side to side from the horse underneath. The last few hours passed in a haze. She swam in her thoughts, the water getting more tumultuous the closer they got to Nymeria.

"I'm looking at sat feeds for the area," David notified the team. "Most of the ground fighting is taking place on the east side. Brightwater troops have dug in and are separated from the larger Svarthold army. Nymerian police are stretched thin, mostly focused on evacuation."

"So the south side of town is open?" Hailey inquired.

"For the most part. The Blackhats have drop pods, so they can theoretically be anywhere, but most of the fighting is taking place in the east and center of town. Svarthold banners still fly on the keep."

They began passing rural buildings and homesteads outside of the larger city. Most were abandoned, with only the occasional flick of a bystander peeking out from behind a corner or a window. Roads began to coalesce beneath them, signaling the growing presence of a city.

Every step felt heavier than the last.

"What about the serial killer?" Kenji asked as he closed the gap between them. "Any news?"

David skimmed through info on his tablet for a moment. "Another victim since last night. A woman, like the others. Beheaded," David punctuated with a solemn look at Hailey.

"As disturbing as it is, we can't focus on that right now. We have far larger problems to contend with," Hailey claimed, keeping her focus forward.

Kenji shifted, "So, what's the plan, then?"

"Not a very strong one, to be honest. We have to get into the city, then to the palace, hopefully unnoticed. I need to convince the soldiers to let me pass, then the commanders that I am who I say I am, then my bannermen to, again, *hopefully,* answer the call. If we can get reinforcements to take the pressure of the fleets off us, we can get ours in the air to begin a counterattack."

"You still have a fleet they haven't destroyed?"

"The primary one, yes. It's in the ocean. The navy, I assume, couldn't get it out before the Core fleets had a superior position."

"So, we have a lot of barriers, a few unknown factors, miles of open warzone, and several important people to convince," Kenji recounted. He turned and gave a brief look to Clara, who was too distracted to notice. "Let's get started," he confirmed with a breath.

Hailey could plainly see that he was in love with Clara. *Infatuated may be more accurate,* Hailey thought as she nodded at him, *given that they haven't known each other for very long.* They were her bannermen, and through their service, found a greater purpose than she could have hoped for. Hailey felt like she was smiling.

After another hour of discussion and marching, David's eyes widened as he looked ahead of them, recognizing something Hailey couldn't notice. He broke away from the party with speed and galloped up the hill in front of them and stopped at its pinnacle.

"David!" Hailey called out. "Where are you going? What do you see?" She kicked her horse to a higher speed and raced to meet him. He hadn't answered her questions, hadn't looked in her direction, but only stared into the distance.

Hailey crested the hill and understood David's captivation as it all came into view.

Nymeria.

Still miles away, the sight stole the breath she didn't have. The white stone gleamed a deep orange in the late evening sun. The city seemed a jewel set into the countryside, the landscape a band made to present it.

From their vantage, the breadth of the city proper was visible to them. The low streets, compact and labyrinthine climbed a steady ascent to the high streets, open and tall, until meeting at its apex: the palace. Her home stood like a beacon, towering and strong in the center of the city.

Hailey could see smoke rising from the eastern sides of town, homes cracked open to reveal their interior, towers toppled into what were once clean and breezy streets. The occasional pops of gunfire and explosions reached them, despite the distance.

From the western and north-western gates poured refugees. They formed lines and carried their lives on their backs.

Her home, her people, needed her, and with renewed resolve, she steeled herself against this challenge.

Daughter of my father.

KENJI KARAKURA

Disheveled and scared, the guard stood between them and the rest of the city. His exhaustion momentarily pushed aside at the sight of the six beings on five horses requesting passage into Nymeria.

"The city is under siege. Why the hell would you want to go inside?" he asked, his voice hoarse.

Hailey sighed and conceded, "Because I am Hailey Svarthold, rightful Lord of Arcturus and the Outer Reach."

The man stared blankly for a moment, then rolled his eyes. "Alright, get out of here," he made a shooing motion, "before I tell the Paladins there's some weird AI person running around."

"What's your name?"

"Don't worry about it."

"I won't, but I'm sure Sir Gerard will." The guard's eyebrows furrowed. "He is still your boss, yes? I'm guessing he's in charge during this siege. Why don't you tell him that there's a Svarthold at the gates? If that doesn't do it for you," Hailey turned on her horse and pointed at Kenji, "that is Kenji Karakura, Rear Admiral of the Karakura navy and nephew to the Lord of the Inner Reach. You remember how they came to our aid in a time of need, yes?" Kenji did his best to hold a modest, solemn expression befitting authority. "In fact, we have all manner of noble families here with me. Hill, Brightwater, and Yamada. Now get your ass on the radio and let them all know your Lord has returned."

The man stood still, calculating. After a moment, he reached into his cloak with a sigh and retrieved his tablet.

"Sergeant Willoby, southern guard post, sir... Yes, we have six individuals requesting entry... Yes sir, I told them..." The group shot each other quick glances that all said, '*I hope this works*,' in silent unison. "Well, one of them claims to be Hailey Svarthold... Yes sir, she states she isn't actually dead... Correct... She's also here with members of the families Hill, Brightwater, uh Yamada and Karakura. And some little non-human. Yes sir, Kenji Karakura... Of course, here she is." Willoby handed his tablet over to Hailey

On the display was a stout, older man, whom Kenji assumed was Sir Gerard.

"You have to be kidding me," Sir Gerard began.

"Gerry, hold on, I know how this looks. Give me two minutes to explain. I promise you, it's me."

Hailey recounted her tale to Sir Gerard, leaving nothing out. Some details were still unknown to Kenji; the nature of Henry's death, the time spent on Argon, the quick trip to Titan. There were details about her growing up in the city that only she would know, like when she ran away at a young age and how Sir Gerard embraced her on her return at the hands of the Halloway family. "All that to say: it worked. Henry got the technology working and that's why I'm here."

Sir Gerard remained silent for an uncomfortable length of time. Kenji watched the knight on screen as he began to shift in thought. Sir Gerard's hard visage melted, and he started to choke up. "I mourned you."

Hailey bowed her head in shame. "I'm so sorry, Gerry," she responded in a whisper.

Sir Gerard sniffed and wiped his nose. "If this is some trick from the Glassers, I swear I won't stop until Armand Glasser is dead at my hand."

"Together, Gerry, we're going to fulfil that promise."

"Please come to the palace and we'll see if there's something we can do about these pests in our city."

Hailey handed the tablet back to Sergeant Willoby as she sauntered by, her friends following suit, finally in Nymeria.

The southern portion of the city was relatively untouched, but the occasional scar of war appeared on the streets they walked; empty homes, doors and shutters left flapping in the breeze, luggage and belongings abandoned on the streets in haste. They moved through serpentine streets, up winding hills and through town squares and saw no one. Apart from the cracks in the distance, all they heard were the footfalls of the horses beneath them and the wind that whipped through the alleyways.

"This way." Hailey guided them toward the palace. "If we cut up through high town, we should be able to get to the gardens before it gets dark."

Kenji watched Clara, apart from herself and deep in thought, as she had been for hours. He opened his mouth to ask if something was wrong just as she galloped to the head of the party to Hailey.

"Hailey, I need to tell you something."

"What is it?" Worry tinged Hailey's voice.

"I've... I made a mistake," Clara admitted, her voice rattling. "I was only doing it to save my family, I promise, I would never have done this to you otherwise."

Hailey slowed her horse to a stop and faced Clara. "Clara, what did you do?" Hailey asked softly, concern giving way to empathy.

"I told the Lords about your father's—"

Clara's words were cut short as she was tackled from the back of her horse. A thin, cloaked figure lunged from an alleyway unseen and dove into her. It wrapped its arms around her neck and was beginning to pull, Clara let out choked screams as it wrenched.

"Clara!" Kenji screamed and dismounted his horse to help. He lunged forward and was met with a swift kick to the chest from the figure as it turned in response. The kick threw Kenji violently into a wall, breaking several of his ribs from its inhuman strength. Kenji slumped against the wall and coughed, barely holding on to consciousness.

The figure seemed a shadow, flowing around Clara and wrapping itself around her neck.

Hailey jumped from horseback to land on top of the creature, but it pulled itself and Clara back in a spin. It kicked Hailey in a similar fashion, sending her down the street.

David scrambled to find a weapon, a tool, anything he could use to help. He found a brick and decided it would be good enough. Takeshi stood frozen.

Clara's eyes showed pure fear as she choked out her last word, "Please." Her hands pointed at Kenji, beckoning him.

The hooded figure twisted, and with a sickening crack, Clara's limbs went limp.

It began pulling on her head, as if trying to pry it from her shoulders, when it was hit with a brick in the back of the head, thrown by David. It released Clara's body and allowed her to fall to the ground. It turned to look at David.

Kenji was swimming in his own head, the surrounding city a blur of concussed senses and immense pain. Struggling to breathe, he began crawling to Clara.

David backed slowly as the figure approached with intimidating torpidity. "Hopper, run!" David yelled as he put up fists.

The figure was sent sideways from a kick from Hailey. The strength of her form matching its own. "Get up the hill! Get help!" she screamed to David. "GO!"

The figure lifted itself from the ground, its cloak in tatters. The hood was down, and Hailey saw its face. Though it had human features, artificial skin, and blond hair, it looked uncanny as it stared blankly at her with unnaturally blue eyes. It began marching at her as David, Takeshi and Hopper mounted horses and galloped away.

Kenji reached Clara, lifeless upon the side of the road. Fear still clung to her open eyes as he brushed her hair from her face.

Hailey lunged forward with a quick left-hand strike followed by a wide right punch. Both hits made solid contact, causing it to double back, but it quickly regained its posture and counter attacked.

A flurry of blows hit Hailey as it pushed forward, wild strikes from alternating hands hitting Hailey in the arms she put up to defend her face.

She couldn't see as it pressed its attack and finished the long chain of swipes with another kick, sending Hailey back down the street. It wasted no time and ran down the street to meet her on the ground, so swift in its steps that it seemed to float.

While Hailey was lying on her back, she put up a foot in defense, with which the figure made abrupt contact. Using its momentum, Hailey flipped it over her head. She stood and charged, releasing a scream that seemed to break up her vocal monitor.

The figure rose to one knee before Hailey closed the distance and struck it in the head viciously. Kenji could hear the low clang of the battle ringing off the tall, white buildings, as though the echoes themselves were in conflict.

Hailey threw another right hook, but her arm was caught underneath its left, locking it in place. Hailey stood eye to blank face with the entity for a breath of a moment before it struck her in the chest. It struck repeatedly; three times before she could raise an arm in defense. With the last punch, it released her, using the power of the hit to send her prone once more.

Before Hailey could defend herself, it wrapped its arms around her neck and rotated behind her. It began wrenching in the same way it had done with Clara. Hailey struggled, writhed and clawed; she sent elbows and punches backward, but they all landed flat. It only pulled harder, twisting further as she panicked.

Kenji felt a tide of black washing over him as he began to lose consciousness.

A sudden crack startled Kenji. He looked at the figure and noticed that it had separated from Hailey, and she was still intact. A smoking hole in its chest became visible as it rose to meet a new challenge. Hailey scrambled up and over to Kenji's side.

Kenji could see someone new down the street. The man held a glaive, his cloak billowed behind him. An energy shield burst to life on his left arm as he stood in response to this threat.

A paladin of the Order of the Lesser.

SIMON CANSBY

"Arms up!" Avery yelled before striking another time, pushing Simon off his balance. He let out a grunt as he hit the padded floor. "You can see now why footing is important." Avery reached out his arm to pick Simon up off the training room floor. Simon grabbed hold and lifted himself upward, ready to try again. "Your shield is a tool," Avery instructed, "and it is nothing if you aren't planted. The strength of the tower is in its foundations."

"Hit the kill switch! NOW!" Simon screamed down the Nymerian street to Damir. The young man pressed a button on his tablet and looked onward for a response.

The Rakshasa paused in its step and shuddered, the hole in its chest still smoldering. Simon saw a break in the perpetual onslaught of tests against his resolve. He almost let a smile break across his face.

The Rakshasa stopped shaking and matched Simon's gaze with a blank, lifeless one, and continued to walk forward.

"Why isn't it shutting down, Damir?" Simon asked, urgently.

Damir shook his head and looked back and forth between his tablet and the Rakshasa. "No, no, no, no."

"Damir!"

"It's bypassed my programming!"

Simon knew a smile was too eager in hindsight. He put his arms up and set his foundation, his feet shoulder's width apart.

The Rakshasa lunged forward, swiping left and right at Simon. With his shield lifted to guard, he deflected the blows as they bounced off the hard light with high-pitched pings. Simon riposted, thrusting forward with his glaive above his shield, stabbing the Rakshasa in the neck.

There was no blood.

It jumped back and readied itself for another attack.

"There will be times where our foundation won't be strong enough." Avery circled the training room around Simon. *"What do we do in these situations?"*

"We parry, Sir Rohan."

"Correct." Avery flashed a quick smile; focus forward as he walked in circles around the room. *"We use their momentum and push the attack aside. It can be risky, so you must learn to time it correctly."*

Simon stood as a wall against the creature before him; shield ready, glaive above and pointed forward.

The Rakshasa pounced, swift and intimidating. It crossed the ground between them in the blink of an eye, its kick poised to hit Simon in the center of his shield.

Simon thrust his shield to the left, catching the Rakshasa in the foot and sending it off-balance, and it fell to one knee. In the momentary pause, Simon trained the point of the glaive on its face and released another shot. Shrapnel and fake flesh sheared away from the Rakshasa's head, sending it up the cobblestone street, and it doubled over.

"Your shield is versatile," Avery instructed. *"It can change shape. Like so."* He flexed the last two fingers on

his left hand and the shield shifted from a standard half-guard to a tower shield, almost as tall as he was. Avery pointed his training glaive forward, held above the shield, at Simon. Impenetrable and pointed, simultaneous attack and defense, all at the push of a button. "It can take on any shape you can think of. The only limit is your imagination."

The Rakshasa lifted its hollow visage, a third of its face missing, to meet Simon's eyes with only one of its own. Fiber optic wires and fragments of metal from inside its head met the light of day as it kneeled in the street.

Simon saw an emptiness behind its eye and wondered how similar he might be to something like this; if it feels, wants or needs. *Is it bound by its programming only, or are there other forces driving its decisions?* Simon thought as he remembered what he had left behind that he desired so intensely. *Come back to me.*

The Rakshasa lurched and drove its pointed hand into Simon's side like a knife. Simon screamed and swung his glaive down in response, only for it to be caught in the Rakshasa's other hand.

In a stalemate, the two stared at each other as the Rakshasa lifted itself back to its feet. It began twisting its hand and Simon screamed louder, blood beginning to soak his cloak and armor.

Simon flexed the last two fingers of his left hand, and his shield shapeshifted from a half-guard shield to a pointed dagger protruding from his knuckles.

Simon punched hard and drove the dagger deep into what remained of its head, wrenching it to the side. The Rakshasa ripped its hand from Simon's side, leaving an open wound pouring blood at an alarming rate, and loosened its grip on the glaive.

Simon jumped back and slashed simultaneously, catching the Rakshasa above the collarbone, cleaving into its chest. It fell once again to its knees, its left arm seemingly inoperable.

It stared at Simon vacantly. Simon stared back with a snarl, breathing heavily.

"The galaxy is replete with things that want you dead, Simon." Abvery explained, the two of them taking a break from training. "If I can teach you anything it's this: always keep humility in your heart. Always strive to be the good you want to see in the galaxy." Avery's tone went from soft to stern as he turned his head to look Simon in the eye. "But if someone forces you to defend yourself, put them down hard, and make sure they don't get back up."

With a yell, Simon pulled the glaive out and struck the Rakshasa again. Then again. Simon repeatedly slashed his foe and screamed, releasing all fear and adrenaline. He didn't stop until the machine laid before him in pieces.

Panting, he stumbled backward and turned to look at the mechanical horses galloping away up the street. They had just loaded their dead friend on one while the injured one struggled to stay on another. Damir rushed forward to Simon's side once the threat had been eliminated.

Then Simon saw her plain: her brushed steel, featureless face, the brown robes that had the dust of the planet where he first saw her still clinging to it. She looked at him briefly, then turned the horse and rode away.

Simon knew then that he had saved the last Svarthold.

He collapsed, reality going black around him.

TO MAKE PROGRESS

CLARA BRIGHTWATER

If you're hearing this, then I've died, and you've rummaged through my things. I don't blame you; there are a lot of things I've been meaning to say, but to begin: my journey thus far has been something I never could have imagined.

To set the picture straight, I'll start with my time on the planet Eidolon. Not my entire history, of course. I think this thing only has an hour of recording time, at best.

Anyways, I am... was third in line for lordship. The territory consisted of two minor quadrants that... I don't need to explain this to you, Hailey. I just hope it wasn't you that killed me. Though, I would understand.

I found out about Henry conducting his experiments on human consciousness and remembered my family's legacy with the Svartholds; specifically, how we have been loyal for generations. The Brightwaters were stewards to the Svartholds during the later conquest, and gifted lordship and titles by Gregar Svarthold after years of service.

I remember the dinner I had the same night I received the news about Henry. My older brother had just received a scholarship with the upper echelon of the Cidrius academy to become a professor, my younger brother would be leaving to the Galactic Commons to start a career in economics. My eldest brother was, obviously, being groomed to be the next lord of Eidolon. I also learned of my cousin's fortune, and how he would be accepted into the academy for Imperial Sentinels.

All this to say: that same dinner I learned of your father's blasphemy and of my own inconsequence.

In almost the same sentence, my parents mentioned how he had betrayed the empire, forgetting everything the Svartholds had done for our family, followed by a mention of my marriage to someone I'd never met, all in the means of an attempt to cut taxes for the same empire to which they proclaimed loyalty.

My brothers were leaving to do *great things,* and I was to become a farm to be traded; a form of currency exchanging hands. What was the point of me becoming an expert in microbiology and neurology? All the time I spent studying. For what?

Sorry, I've been feeling introspective; hence the recording. Kenji said something to me earlier that resonated, and I've been having trouble shaking it. '*Things, otherwise unnoticed, seem to manifest only in hindsight,*' is what he told me.

Anyways, I was forced, even though I would have loved to work with him on my own accord, to follow Henry around and give intel on his whereabouts.

A private message reached me one morning explaining that Henry was looking for research assistants, on a clandestine channel, of course. He had already left Arcturus at this point.

I ruminated on the option for days. I knew it would be a huge risk for not only my career, but my life in general. The risks of upsetting one's appearance to the empire was enough to keep me away. I could be exiled from my sector. Thousands of lightyears of space that I would never again be allowed to enter, and that's the best-case scenario.

My thoughts went in the dissenting direction, however. I heard the call and was drawn like a sailor to a siren; to be something when the universe is almost entirely nothing seemed impossible, as Henry put it, and that thought was enthralling.

Still, I had withdrawn from the position, knowing in my heart that I just wasn't strong enough to upset the way of things. At the time, I couldn't imagine my mother's disappointment; couldn't bear to conjure the picture of her face when presented with the news that I had become a traitor and a fugitive. Now, I only want to see her again and tell her I'm sorry.

I had, unfortunately, made my presence known to whomever was watching in my first interaction with Henry's enquiry for research assistants.

My cousin, the one that was accepted into the Imperial Sentinels, was the first target. He had divulged some information about my family; not exactly sure what, but it caught the eyes and ears of imperial intelligence. They sent a cryptic message explaining the peril in which he might be put, depending on his *assignment*. They made it clear that the decision for his assignment would be dependent on my cooperation.

The next target was Eugene Brightwater of the Council of Scholars. Apparently planting *irrefutable evidence of corruption* would be all too easy; they sent me a video of him mid-ritual, the nature of which I don't know, but it looked like the highly illegal kind of arcane practice.

I'm still unsure how true that one might be.

The third target was my brother, Clide. The one who had just begun his economic studies on Titan.

They sent me a video of him sleeping.

And so, it was decided that I would depart in the night and join your father in his research.

A large portion of it was completed by the time I had joined the team, consisting mostly of decades of work while he was the Lord of the Outer Reach.

I met David Hill on Argon, where we took a ferry to B-115. I had never met a Carthian before this, and the interaction was... surprising to say the least.

I've come to truly enjoy my time with Hopper, though I'm not sure just how much of my intention he captured in my time with him. I did everything I could to cover the truth in my mind, to the point where I was starting to believe all the lies I was creating to justify my actions.

David became a fast friend during our work together, as well. There were a few all-nighters and heated discussions about how best to integrate biology and technology. 'A *Hill knows where his honor lies*,' I heard him say more than once. Upon some thought at that, I became disappointed in my own family; they didn't know that the Empire to which they were loyal had a gun to their head.

Then there was Henry; his work was so foundational to my own career that I had, on several occasions, daydreamed about sitting down and interviewing him, coming up with topics and responses to questions never asked. All forgotten when face-to-face with the man.

After all my time at the Cidrius Academy, following the work of the intellectual and lord, here he was with sunken eyes and dirty clothes, bedraggled and tired. He hovered over an android body, into which he poured his entire person; a living sacrifice engendering resurrection.

I felt the anxiety when we first switched you on, Hailey; the wonder and dread of realizing that I was standing right in the middle of history being made. Everything I could have ever wanted, all at the cost of everything else.

Once we lost Henry, I thought imperial intelligence would leave me alone; that my part in this ruse was over.

For a short while, there was radio silence, and relief started to settle on my mind like a gentle snow, but that didn't last long. On our way to Titan, I was asked for an update. I tried to keep the details as vague as possible, but I think they saw through that. I had to let them know where we were going after we left for Arcturus.

It was pretty fortuitous, actually. Had we stayed on Titan, it would have been all too easy for the Sentinels to capture you.

The truth is eating away at me, I'm not sure how much longer I can continue before I blurt it out in the middle of a conversation. At the very least, I hope you can hear this and know that you truly were my friends.

Here goes.

It is to you, David, that I issue my first apology. I feel as though we could have been life-long friends. I was envious of your steadfast faith in what you were doing and the picture of honor and loyalty that was so clear to you. You taught me a lot.

Hopper, I am sorry for never communicating with you in an honest and open way. In making my mind unreadable, it was like I was lying to you every second of every day.

Hailey... nothing I say will convey just how sorry I am. I still don't know if we did the right thing by bringing you back to life. I've been contemplating whether I should tell you about my treachery, and whether that will do any of us any good. Would it be better for you to hear it now? Whit looking down at my corpse? Or should I say it to you in person, so you can see me say it, so you can look in my eyes and know what it's been doing to me?

I guess we'll see.

I've grown to respect you in every way. I hope you can get back to your people and make a real difference. I hope that your influence will offset the things I've done.

HAILEY SVARTHOLD

"Kenji," Clara's voice played on her tablet, bouncing off the white stone walls of the palace in the center of Nymeria, "I think under different circumstances, I would have loved to see where this goes. So, my last apology is to you. I'm sorry we don't have more time to spend together. Good luck, everyone."

The recording ended. Hailey stood over Clara's body, covered in a white sheet, as she had guessed in the recording. David and Hopper stood by her, still silent as though they were waiting for her voice to chime again. David's pensive look hung on his face, changing to grief as the reality of the situation slowly took hold.

"I think we should wait for Kenji to recover," David choked out finally, "before giving this to him."

Hailey responded with a curt nod. "So, this is what she was trying to tell me, then. Right before..."

David mirrored Hailey's nod. The three stood thinking as Sir Gerard entered the room, followed closely by another. "Here he is, my lord." The qualifier took Hailey by surprise. *Right, me. Lord.* The man following Gerard wore blue armor, covered in stains of dirt, ash, oil, and blood. With dark brown hair and piercing blue eyes, Hailey could see the resemblance. "Captain Alister Brightwater," Gerard announced.

"Captain," Hailey began, "I know this looks strange, but I am Hailey Svarthold, Lord of Arcturus and the Outer Reach."

The captain's eyes darted uncertainly between her and Gerard. He issued a hesitant bow and said, "My lord."

"Thank you for what you've done for my city. You and your soldiers have shown strength and loyalty that will not be forgotten."

"Of course, my lord. I apologize for the rest of my family, I was only able to secure a small force when the news of your father came to us."

"I understand. The circumstances are... trying."

"If I may ask, why am I here? My men need me. Blackhat divers are hitting us on all sides."

Hailey looked down to the covered body lying next to her.

"Who is that?" he asked, voice starting to shake.

"This is Clara Brightwater." Alister stared blankly for a few moments, almost as though he couldn't understand what was being said. He began stepping forward slowly, like he was afraid the sound of his footsteps would wake the body in front of him. He gently lifted the white sheet and seemed shocked to confirm Hailey was telling the truth. The frequency of his breathing increased as he stared into familiar, cold blue eyes. Alister replaced the sheet and closed his own eyes, gathering himself. "She died in service to me and the Svarthold legacy. I wouldn't be here now if not for her work; the Svarthold line ended," Hailey explained. Alister's eyes opened and remained fixed on Clara's covered silhouette. Hailey continued, "I'm afraid I need to ask more of you."

His gaze snapped to Hailey. "More than this?" he motioned to Clara on the table. "More than what the Brightwaters have already given you? I've lost brothers in defense of this city. An unquantifiable sacrifice for a legacy I wasn't sure still existed. Now we have...

something *telling us* that she's really a woman that died months ago. How convenient; a legacy reborn?"

"Mind your tone, Captain!" Gerard bellowed. Hailey responded with a soft wave in his direction, signaling for repose.

"Alister," Hailey began. "I have asked myself the same thing. You and your family have already given so much, without a moment to grieve. Now, some metal imposter strides through and claims the Outer Reach. The absurdity is not lost on me, Captain. That aside, why would these people shepherd me home if I am not who I say I am?"

"I've been with her every step of the way," David cut in. "I watched her come back to life with my own eyes."

"If ever you've had faith in the Svartholds, I ask you to call upon it now. If ever you've had faith in Sir Gerard, the Hills, the Karakuras. If ever you've had faith in Clara. Call upon it now, like they have."

They could only hear low, steady breathing as Alister calculated to himself, the silent ambience augmented by the white stone around them. Alister let out a brief sigh, "What would you have me do?" he asked, frustrated as he pinched the bridge of his nose.

"Bring her home," Hailey stated softly. "Let your family know what she's done. Let her be put to rest in the ways befitting a Brightwater." She moved to rest a hand on Clara's arm. "Clara made a recording, shortly before she passed. Almost clairvoyantly. It details how the emperor had forced her to betray her family under duress. I tell you this because the Karakura fleet was destroyed by imperial ships, clearly pointing at collusion between the Lords of the Core and the emperor. We need this message to reach the other great houses. We need your help to get reinforcements to Arcturus and push back this Core fleet."

"To what end?" Alister asked poignantly. "That's the first pebble in a landslide. The only way this ends is in civil war. The *EMPEROR* is playing favorites among the great houses? If I'm even a little bit upset by this news, then I can think of three other lords that are *furious*."

"So are we just standing by and doing nothing? Am I just to stand down and die in the name of the status quo? Is that the end your men want after all they've given? Is that the end Clara would want?"

"STOP!" Alister snapped. In the pocket of silence he created, he began to pace. "That's not what I'm saying, I just need you to understand the weight of what *you're* saying. There's no way this ends without blood."

"I don't think it *continues* without blood, either. Alister, he destroyed the *entire* fifth fleet of the Karakuras. Thousands dead in seconds. Imagine if the emperor is left to act freely, without oversight or accountability. How long until he's turning whole planets into glass?"

The ground rumbled from a nearby explosion, punctuating the conversation and reminding them of their perilous surroundings.

"I can't leave my men," Alister stated matter-of-factly. "If we were to retreat, the palace would be taken inside a day. Without reinforcements, I won't be able to leave. You'll need a different agent for this."

"I don't have anyone else."

"Yes, you do," David claimed.

"David, after everything, I can't ask this of you, too."

"We're at the finish line, here, and, like you said, you don't have anyone else. I would be offended if you didn't ask." David flashed a wry half smile. "Let me do this. I'll reach out to my family as well. Maybe even get hold of the Kopeshes, Swimmers and Forgemans. Hell, I might even be so brave as to ask the Falconers." David stepped forward and placed a hand on Hailey's shoulder. "Let me take her home. Let me call your banners."

SIMON CANSBY

"-Over here—"

"-Heavy as hell, Simon, what've you been—"

"-Citadel. The small med bay, around the corner. Yes, the false wall. Turn—"

"-Sure if you can hear me, Simon, but this should—"

Lightning struck Simon in the chest and he woke in an instant, gasping for more air than he felt his lungs could take in. A wave of rage and uncertainty washed over him as he tried to get up from the med bay table, thrashing his limbs.

"Simon! Hey hey hey, it's me, buddy, it's Bill." Bill attempted to hold Simon against the table as he came to. Damir stood beside him with a large, empty syringe, his eyes wide and red.

Simon stopped thrashing and looked around rapidly, his breaths frequent and shallow. "*Where am I?*"

"Onboard the Persistence. You're safe, you got the guy," Bill affirmed.

Simon looked down at his side, covered in blood, soaking from his armpit to his thigh. The pain rushed back like it was late to the conversation. Simon craned his head back and winced in response.

"We had to hit you with an ephrinaline shot to keep you from going into a coma. How'd it feel? I've heard people call it bottled lightning," Bill said with a chuckle.

"I'd say that's exactly what it felt like," Simon gasped, with a weak smile. He took a few moments to catch his breath, then asked, "How did you guys know I was going into a coma?"

Bill looked to Damir, who shrugged. "What do you mean?" Bill asked him, taken aback. "You said he was gonna go into a coma or something!"

"I said we were lucky he wasn't put into a coma, then you handed me this needle and told me to stab him in the chest."

"Well," Bill began waving his arms around, "I d-... He could've... Fuck, Simon are you ok?"

Simon fell back to the med bay table and let out a sigh. *At least I can be done with this mission,* he thought. *I've accomplished far more than they've asked of me.* Simon was excited to finally rest.

"I think I'll be alright once we close this hole in my side," he answered without opening his eyes.

"We'll get it mended, but you're going to need further attention once we're back on Harbor. All I can really muster up on the Persistence is a patch job."

"It'll have to do, then."

The Persistence began its journey to the Pyli Trebuchet, shortly after Bill and Damir had painfully sewn Simon back together. Most of his armor was ruined, but Simon thought that, without it, he may not be alive.

He spent the ride back in the Citadel - the hidden med bay. It also housed the ship's food supplies so that, in the case of enemy boarding, the crew had a place to hold out. Bill was a fan of old humanity history, which was why he called this room the Citadel. '*The trade ships and privateers that would sail the oceans of Earth always had a citadel in case they were boarded by pirates,*' he had told Simon when they first met, whilst he was giving the official tour of the ship. '*I even had the door finished in a way that, when it's closed, you can't even tell it's there.*' Bill had closed the door and a panel dropped down from the ceiling to cover it. '*Pretty neat, right?*' Bill's grin glowed as he looked at Simon. Simon could tell he loved the ship and all its quirks. '*I have a bunch of fail-safes hard wired into the ship. All custom, all off the books. That's the benefit of being a private contractor.*' Harbrand was never told about the secret room or any of the other fail-safes; Bill trusted Simon with some, but not all, of his secrets. '*Hell, I can even vent the entire cabin into space from the cockpit. A last gift from ol' Bill if anyone manages to take the ship from me. Sure, it'll kill me in the process, but I'll take every one of the bastards with me.*' He had chuckled and put his hands on his hips as he smiled and admired his beloved Persistence.

Damir would occasionally keep him company, though the two found little in common with one another. Simon felt guilty as he admittedly didn't try very hard; he recovered from his wound and was often too tired.

Simon's curiosity was eventually piqued, however.

"How much of this was the emperor?" Simon asked abruptly, catching Damir off guard. Damir flashed an inquisitive look; the question seemed to be too vague for him to understand. "The Karakura fleet, I got that much," Simon elaborated, "but how much more? What else has he done? How big of a conspiracy are we exposing?"

Damir looked to the floor and sighed. "I don't know."

"You had a front seat, what do you mean you don't know?"

"I don't know how deep this goes. I was far too busy. I was in charge of research into the... the engram." Simon looked at him from behind furrowed brows. "So, I never had much time away from my lab."

"Back up, what engram?"

"The Svarthold engram. How Henry Svarthold brought back his daughter."

"How were you studying it? Hailey is still running around out there."

"Henry resurrected another person in the Barcelona system. He was killed by a paladin, so we grabbed the body to study it. The problem is that the engram is stored in the head and the body had its—"

"Head blown off," Simon interrupted.

"Correct... how did you know?"

"I was the paladin that blew his head off." Damir paused, staring blankly, until he began laughing; guttural and hearty, tears showing in his eyes. Simon laughed with him for a moment, but didn't find the situation *that* funny. "What?" Simon asked, perturbed, after a few more moments of uninterrupted hysteria.

"I can't tell you just how angry I've been at you," Damir explained through intermittent chuckles. "I was expected to create a working version of the engram for my superior, otherwise *I expected* I was going to die. I would never have guessed the person that caused me the most frustration in my entire life would be my salvation." He settled down and wiped the tears away with a smile. "Life can be strange at times."

Simon silently appreciated the statement, *my salvation.*

"Ok, you had an informant on the inside, so that's how you knew about the Magistrate once I killed him, but how did the emperor know about Henry's work at all?"

"Is that what they called him?" Damir scoffed. "The emperor knew about it for a long time, I suspect, ever since Henry filed for a patent on the technology. I was told that the problem was created by the Order. Henry was warned to stop his research into the engram by a paladin, so he continued his research in secret. Once his daughter died, he went into hiding so he could bring her back. I think the emperor knew the entire time and allowed it to continue. Do you know how easy it is for imperial intelligence to track a lord of one of the great houses?"

"For what, though? And how does it tie to the Lords of the Core?"

"I am one of the very few in the last hundred years to create a completely sentient artificial intelligence. The emperor didn't know this, or else I'd be dead, but my superiors knew. They proposed that they had experts that could 'solve the problem,' as it were. From there it was just a matter of incentive. To swoop in and take territory that had been abandoned by its lord seemed all too easy, so the emperor promised to assist in exchange for an engram."

"What does the emperor want with the engram technology?"

"That's the simplest part. Immortality."

"What about his endless legacy? If we keep creating the same emperor over and over again, what difference does it make?"

"This Desmond wants to be the last one." Damir responded with a shrug. The two sat for a moment in quiet reflection; the weight of their respective circumstances suffusing with their bones. "Really, your order was the wild card in the whole plot. The emperor couldn't directly command the Order of the Lesser to cease investigation into what is essentially your jurisdiction. If you hadn't intervened, the need for the emperor to exchange a throneworld for my services may not have been necessary."

Simon smirked. His humility stifled at the thought of an interminably large machine being broken by him throwing so small a wrench.

Until he added everything up and the smirk slowly faded.

"*Your* services?"

"Yes, like I said, I'm one of the very few that could have solved this problem."

"Now *you* have stolen away."

"Right." Damir seemed to notice Simon's face turn stony once again. "What?"

Simon sighed deeply. "How long do we have?"

"Until what?"

"Until they come looking for you."

"They wouldn't dare attack a paladin. Once we've arrived on Harbor, we'll have complete diplomatic immunity from the Order."

"Press the intercom," Simon instructed, pointing with his head to the screen on the wall beside Damir. Damir reached up hesitantly and tapped the screen. "Bill," Simon called, "how long until we're at the trebuchet?"

"Hey! Glad you're feelin' better, bud. Looks like we've still got a little over three hours."

"Can you please send out a long-range ping to see if we're being followed?"

"Sure... there. If we don't hear back within a half hour, we're clear. Anything beyond that is too far to follow."

"Thanks, Bill."

Damir released his hand from the screen. "You think they'll come for us before we can get to Harbor?"

"Do you have any doubt? It would be easy for them to deny; '*The paladin questioned us, then flew down to Arcturus. We never heard from him again.*' You're telling me you couldn't see your superiors telling that lie like it wasn't second nature to them?"

Damir stared into the middle distance, his eyes fluttering. "What do we do?"

"Sit and hope that ping doesn't come back within a half hour."

A loud clang sounded from the door to the Citadel. It had been locked. Simon motioned to the screen and Damir activated the intercom.

"Bill, why did you lock us in here?"

"It was a good call to send out that ping, Simon, just looks like we were too late." *The signal came back fast,* Simon thought, *they're close.* "Locking you in there in case we're boarded. They won't be able to find you."

"How long do we have?"

"Twenty minutes."

"No chance of outrunning it?"

"We're already flying close to max right now."

"What colors are they flying?"

"It says it's a trading vessel, but I don't buy it with how fast it's moving."

Damir perked up, "What's the ship's signature?"

"It's uhh... one sec... BH-141-ELS-1. Why?"

Damir looked slowly, sullenly to Simon. "It's a Blackhat Hunter-Killer."

KENJI KARAKURA

Wind scoured the bluff.
He allowed it to be him,
And all he needed.
When she asked him a question
He could only hear the wind.

Kenji tilted his head like a dog in response to an enquiry muffled by what he hoped was the gale along the coast, but knew it was deep reflection holding his attention.

She smiled, and it was the perfect smile. Her hair was being gently swept eastward by the winds off the coast, her eyes shone bluer against the grey of the overcast sky, her cheeks blushed red from the cold.

Kenji looked from her to the coastline, one he knew, on the planet Torii, where he had once felt at home. He looked back from the coast, and into his future; the woman whose smile enchanted him.

He held her hand; at once presented with the home he wanted to return to, and the person with which he wanted to return.

Kenji woke, his outstretched hand cold above the blankets.

Nearby, Takeshi Yamada slept in a chair, snoring as his chin rested against his chest. Kenji lifted his head slightly to look about the room. He assumed he was in a medical center in Nymeria, judging by the white walls and machines plugged into him. He shifted and pain erupted from his ribcage. Kenji winced but fought through to elevate himself against his pillows.

"Where is everyone?"

Takeshi released a violent snort as he stirred. "You're awake!" Kenji smiled weakly in response as Takeshi rose from his chair. "How are you feeling?"

Kenji winced again. "Not great, but I'm breathing."

"I'll let the doctors know you're awake." Takeshi turned to leave.

"Wait. Did everybody make it?"

Takeshi dipped his head. "I'll uh... I'll grab Hailey as well. She said she wanted to speak to you."

Kenji's heart sank as the door closed behind Takeshi. *You couldn't save her,* he berated himself, *you couldn't save your people aboard the Maelstrom and you couldn't save the one person who started to mean something to you.*

He spiraled for a few more minutes before Hailey poked her head in through the door. "Kenji?"

"I should've died on the Maelstrom." Hailey paused at the doorway. "I should have died in the line of duty. At least that way I wouldn't have fallen in love and been too weak to do anything about it. I wouldn't have had to watch her die."

"I should be dead, too," Hailey related as she took a light step forward. "I've been curious what it will actually be like... and whether I'll get the opportunity to know what death is."

"She reached out to me. The last thing she saw was a man too spineless to serve his duty. Too fragile to protect her."

"*Or* the last thing she saw was a person that cared about her." Hailey gently sat bedside. "Kenji, that thing almost killed a paladin. I saw him bleeding as he struck it down, just before we ran. It almost took my head off. We're lucky to be alive, and you charged at it without hesitating."

"I have nothing. My family will consider me a coward when they learn that I'm alive. Clara was the one glimmer of light in an otherwise starless existence."

"Are you sure your family will consider you a coward?"

"What do you mean? Of course! I escaped and hid in a breach pod. As far as I know, Takeshi and I are the only survivors of the entire fifth fleet."

"Well, from my point of view, it looks like you continued the mission."

Kenji turned his reddening eyes up to Hailey. "What?"

"Your family came here to assist the Svartholds. Even after you lost everything, you pressed forward to help me on my journey back home. To me, that sounds like dedication to the mission; it sounds like loyalty."

"That leaves out the fact that I hid."

"That doesn't change anything. You're here now, you've been here. How we found each other is inconsequential."

Kenji slumped his head.

The overworked doctor shuffled through the door, followed by Takeshi. Kenji noticed the bags under his eyes as he approached; a clear sign that things hadn't been going well on the front.

"Hello, Kenji. I'm Dr. Lanswell." The tall doctor had a medical face mask and a combat helmet that he removed as he introduced himself.

Hailey stood and maneuvered to the doorway. "I should let him work. Please let me know if you need anything."

Kenji nodded to her before she turned and left.

Dr. Lanswell knelt next to Kenji and pulled out a small flashlight.

"Can you tell me your name?" he asked clinically as he flashed the light in Kenji's eyes.

"Kenji Karakura."

"Good. How well can you move your fingers?"

Kenji lifted his cold right hand and flexed the muscles in his fingers. Stiff, but perfectly functional.

"Looks good." He stopped shining the light in Kenji's eyes. "Can you tell me how you got here?"

How did I get here? Kenji stopped to ponder. *Did instinct take over?*

From Kenji's perspective, the only time he ever had any choice in his path was when he entered that breach pod. *Was it duty?* Rigid service was the only path for Karakura nobles; diverting from the path was dishonorable, putting the interests of oneself before the masses was selfish, leaving one's post was deplorable. *Was it fear?*

When he was young, his mother would tell him stories of his relatives; tales of the progenitors of the family that would inspire and bind so many. *How did you get here? Admiration?* She spoke to him of the men that defined their culture, mentioning Kenzo, his great uncle, or Hideki, Kenji's great-great grandfather. Both had died in ways befitting Karakura nobles: in battle; casting themselves upon the fires of war. *Blind faith?*

HOW DID YOU GET HERE?

Is that who I am? Am I supposed to die to have made any difference? Is it only through sacrifice that my life can have any meaning? I followed, walked without purpose, of course I ended up in a strange land, unsure of myself. The journey began in doubt, and it will stay clouded in doubt until I can make my own meaning of it all.

"Kenji?" Dr. Lanswell checked in after Kenji had been staring into nothing. "Are you able to answer the question? How did you get here?"

"I don't know. I was unconscious from the attack. I assume Hailey, Takeshi or David carried me back here."

"Well, it seems like brain damage was kept to a minimum, which is good. Your scans look optimal, but I'd recommend more rest. Both for your ribs and your head. You would do well to try and avoid any undue stress while your brain is healing. I understand that's a bit of a ridiculous request, given the current state of things, but I need you to try, regardless."

"Thank you, Dr. Lanswell."

"Of course. Get some rest, I'll check on you tomorrow." Dr. Lanswell lifted himself from the edge of Kenji's bed and left the room.

"Kenji," Takeshi began once they were alone, "I'm so relieved that you're okay. That thing we fought was so terrifying, I didn't know what to do."

"Neither did I," Kenji admitted.

"I never know what to do."

Kenji, surprised, cocked his head and examined Takeshi. Solemn and downtrodden, he stared at the bed between them.

"Takeshi—"

"How do I do it?" Takeshi's eyes began to water as he interrupted, "I've been met with terrifying circumstances twice now and I only froze. My father was so brave. My brother was aboard the Summit, just forward of the Maelstrom. I haven't heard anything about him." The sudden recollection of his brother seemed to break the levies holding back his sorrow and he began to sob. "I forgot to grieve him. How do I face this? How do I... be brave?"

Kenji reached out and squeezed Takeshi's hand. His jump at the feeling was sign enough that no one had touched him for some time, like how Kenji had felt when Clara had rested her head on his shoulder.

Takeshi lurched forward and wrapped his arms around Kenji and cried into his shoulder. Despite the pain in his ribs, Kenji held him tight; a reminder that he still had at least one person who was there for him. After they separated, the two sat in contemplative silence, allowing their breathing and the steady whir of the medical equipment to paint the air.

"I don't think we were made for this, Takeshi."

HAILEY SVARTHOLD

Dust. An even film will cover everything if no other forces are acted upon it. As long as there are no open windows, no movement of bodies, no upheavals or disturbances, dust will persist. A constant among stillness, like it had been and always will be, ready to settle whenever we do. Patience given form.

Hailey entered her bedroom for the first time since she had been back and noticed the dust that had collected in her absence, blanketing her old belongings like the faintest of snowfalls. Light poured in from the window and framed an inconsequential portion of the wall to her left. That light was given more life from the dust that lingered in the air, forming a visible sideways column that intersected her former living quarters.

An entirely different life, she thought. The memories from this place didn't feel like any she had experienced; they felt closer to the images one crafts when reading a story and imagining the scenery as described by the exposition. They felt distant and fantastical, paired with a hopeless longing.

The room seemed simultaneously larger and smaller than she had remembered it. The former stemmed from the fact that she had been living aboard the Progress, which hadn't been particularly spacious. The latter feeling came from the inevitable recognition of her own growth in relation to the room itself. Her bedroom was beautiful and airy, with white stone walls and dark wood accents lining the floorboards and framing the windows and doors.

Her belongings were exactly where she had left them. Her bed still unmade from the very last time she would ever sleep. Her books were both organized among the case in neat rows, and disorganized, scattered about her desk, chair and bedstand with bookmarks still in them. The toy she constructed when she was younger from computer parts and an old projector, Nova, cobbled together into a vaguely cube shape, sat on her desk, still broken.

"He kept everything exactly as it was." Sir Gerard approached Hailey, seemingly from nowhere, and startled her, causing her to jump. "Woah, sorry about that. I'm quieter than I look," he chuckled lightly.

"It's ok. I'm just distracted." She continued to stare into the bedroom. Gerard leaned against the doorframe and stared with her, both mulling over the unstirred bedroom in silence.

"The hell you raised around this place," Gerard said with a short smile, rolling his eyes.

Hailey looked at him, once again surprised. "What do you mean?" she said with a laugh.

Gerard started to grin. "You were a pain in my ass, girl."

Hailey felt like her eyes would be wide and her smile wider as she reached out and gently punched Gerard in the arm. "You were a pain in my ass, too!"

"*How?*" he asked in disbelief.

"You were the most difficult obstacle to overcome every time I wanted to sneak out of this place." The pair laughed in the doorway of Hailey's childhood bedroom. They let it settle to a chuckle then just a pensive smile.

"There are a couple of things I should show you," Gerard warned. "I hate to cast you headfirst into leadership, but we're hurting, and we need you to step into your father's shoes."

She had been dreading this. After everything she had been through, Hailey was finally here and had no idea what to do.

"An inevitability, huh? Kinda makes a person believe in fate."

"How so?" Gerard asked as they turned and started walking down the hallway away from her bedroom.

"I took the biggest detour just to end up doing exactly what everyone told me I was supposed to do. What the hell was the point? I struggled so much. The people of Nymeria have suffered so much. For what?"

They passed a broken window, glass shards scattered on the ground. They crunched under Hailey's alloy feet.

"Hailey, you shouldn't be thinking about it like that."

"How can I not?"

"There are so many factors that are out of your control; out of everyone's control. Your father, for instance, was one of the most powerful men in the empire, but he couldn't keep his own daughter from sneaking out at night." Hailey felt a sense of bittersweet melancholy at that, a kind of warm sadness. The thought of her father in a huff because she was causing problems again made her glow in self-satisfaction. "And nobody can say whether it was fate or not that led you on that path. There's always the potential that the lessons you've learned are what were intended by whatever Greater had lined up for you." They came to a halt in front of the doors to the throne room, embroidered with the visage of the Svarthold legacy; great spires morphing into double helix structures as they reached upward. "Or there could be no divined path, and our purpose is what we make it."

Purpose.

What is purpose? Not mine, but the idea in general, she thought. *Is it just destiny? Then why have I seen so many believe in purpose but scorn the idea of something as grand as fate or destiny?*

Is it expectation? Then whose? Mine? Or everyone else's? And if that expectation belongs to others, then why is it not their purpose?

Is it only a gentle nudge? So benign and mild as to be mistaken or even overlooked? Is purpose just a clue written on the wall; an arrow pointing down a hallway with many doors?

The tall ornate doors opened with a groan to reveal the Svarthold throne room, the white stone tunneled before her to meet at a zenith at the end of the long room flanked by towering windows. At the opposite end was the throne; grey marble veined with orange agate that glowed in the early evening light.

SIMON CANSBY

"You will have one shot at this," Bill warned over the intercom.

"Unlock the door, Bill."

"Can't do that, bud. You can barely stand. I'm not going to let them take you two. Now, like I said, you'll have one shot at this. Damir said the Blackhats will only leave the pilot on board when they board us."

Simon heard the hard clang of the outboard tunnel forcefully connecting the two ships, *they're here.* "What about the rest of them? What do we do with the ones that board us?"

"Simon, shut up and listen," Bill commanded as Damir stood painfully still and silent, frozen in fear as the two conferred over the intercom. "I have a plan. I'm transferring controls over to you for a hidden thermite probe. Once the boarding party is here, you'll launch the probe and attach it to their cockpit. That'll keep them from following us."

"Ok, but, again, what about everyone *on board?*"

"One last gift from old Bill," he answered stoically as he turned off the intercom.

Simon switched the console screen on the wall to a video feed of the primary quarters and cockpit of the Persistence. The port airlock door opened, and three figures stood in the doorway. All were outfitted in glossy black armor. The two behind wore pressure helmets to seal off their suits. The third man, the leader in front of the other two, had no helmet on. Petrev Blackhat led the boarding party.

Simon used another screen on the console to initiate the probe launch. The onboard camera allowed him to see from the probe's perspective. It floated lifelessly out of the hidden compartment on the belly of the Persistence.

"Hello, gentlemen!" Bill turned in his chair to greet the assailants. "Might I ask, what the fuck?"

Blackhat motioned forward with his chin to the assassin on his right, then pointed at Bill as a command to the one on his left. One stepped forward and began clearing the ship. Silently, he checked corners, aiming his rifle everywhere he looked. The other strode to Bill in certain steps and struck him with the butt of his rifle. The airlock shut behind them as they entered.

Simon jumped as Bill crumpled to the ground beside his chair. Simon's breathing became shallow, and he could feel his face contorting to a snarl.

The probe glided through the silence of space, guided by Simon's hand. It cleared the breadth of the Persistence and began its short journey to the enemy ship. A Kestrel, the same that Simon noticed aboard the Peregrin, hanging like bats.

"Where are they?" Blackhat hissed.

Bill gathered himself and sat on his knees. He sighed and asked, "Really? Do you see anybody here?"

Blackhat nodded at his soldier, who turned and struck Bill again, this time with the back of his armored hand. "I haven't the time for this," Blackhat interrogated.

"The paladin stole one of my own, I want him back. Where are they?"

Bill wiped blood from his mouth. "Again, look around. The ship's not that big."

The Kestrel grew in the view of the probe's camera. Simon directed it forward at a crawl. A heads-up display came to life and showed a trajectory to the hostile craft. Simon needed a few more moments.

"They stayed on Arcturus," Bill informed. "I was told to go back to Harbor."

Blackhat knelt next to Bill. "I've been tracking him. I know he's here, aboard this... pile." The first assassin returned from clearing the ship. He shook his head at Blackhat, who returned his gaze to Bill and whispered, "*Where. Are. They?*"

Simon commanded the probe to open its articulating arms. Directly under the Kestrel, it began hunting for a spot onto which it could latch. The readout on screen displayed a red X indicating that it couldn't stick to the side that it was aimed at. *Dammit.* Simon began searching for another spot below the cockpit. No match. Toward the nose of the ship. No match. Further, now emerging from underneath the ship. No match.

"Look, guys," Bill conceded, "I know you're gonna kill me, regardless." Blackhat sighed and stood up as Bill explained. "Can you at least let me go with a bit of dignity?" He started to stand. "This ship means everything to me. Let me die in the chair." Bill hobbled to his pilot's chair. "And you two," he pointed to the faceless assailants as he limped, "look me in the eye when you do it. Take those fucking helmets off, you cowards."

The one that struck Bill depressurized his helmet and removed it, revealing a man in his twenties. Despite his age, he looked like he had seen a hundred years.

Bill planted himself in his chair.

No match. Again. *The damn ship is too smooth.* Simon started to panic. *You'll have one shot at this.* He maneuvered the probe further up the side of the Kestrel. The cockpit came into view, a single soldier sat inside.

"He's going to see the probe!" Damir whispered urgently.

"You too." Bill pointed at the last assassin, still wearing his helmet. "I thought the Blackhats were the best warriors in the galaxy. You people don't look a man in the eye as you take his life?"

The still obscured assassin looked to Blackhat for instruction. He scowled before nodding begrudgingly.

The helmet depressurized with a hiss and the second soldier revealed his face. He had short black hair and a milky left eye, marked by the scar across it.

Match. The check marks on the display turned green and Simon hit enter. The arms on the probe reached forward and drilled into the glass. The man inside noticed and began speaking rapidly, silent through the camera feed. The arms pulled the body of the probe inward to make contact with the glass. A larger drill at its center burrowed into the glass.

Blackhat put his hand to his ear and turned in the direction of his ship. The two assassins looked around furiously. Bill saw his opportunity.

"The Persistence is yours, Simon!" he yelled into the air before grabbing the control stick on his chair, wrenching it sideways.

The Persistence ripped away from the Kestrel in a wild spin, shearing off the boarding tunnel from the side of the ship. The enemy ship began to roll away, fragments of the tunnel flung away violently.

Despite the upheaval in the cockpit and the soldiers flying around in the sudden movement of the ship, Bill held fast.

Simon hit the ground with a thud, Damir fell next to him. The readout on the screen was still green, the drill on the probe still working through the glass.

Bill reached under the left arm of the chair and pressed a hidden button. The airlock door exploded at the seams and ejected from the ship. The vicious claws of pressurized air ripped everyone out into the great emptiness.

Bill included.

The Persistence continued to spin. Simon yelled through the sudden pain from being tossed around. Damir flailed as he drifted through the air. The console on the wall glowed green, awaiting Simon's final input.

He attempted to stand, but the momentum tossed him from floor to wall to ceiling to wall, each impact felt like another stab in his side. *It can't have been for nothing.*

Simon grabbed a cabinet door that had been opening and shutting intermittently and attempted to stabilize himself. In the camera feed at the other end of the Citadel, the Kestrel corrected its spin and turned to face the Persistence. *It's going to destroy us.*

With everything left in his already weakened frame, Simon wrenched at the cabinet to fling himself toward the console. The room rotated around him like a centrifuge, propelling medical tools and trash in a random scatter as he drifted clumsily through the hidden Citadel.

One hand outstretched, Simon reached, a silent plea with the wall. *Please come closer, please just let me reach you.*

The Persistence continued to move freely from Simon, and his pace slowed, the wall getting no closer, until it began to get further away. Simon flailed; he attempted to grab anything he might use to propel himself just a little further. The walls and floor only feet from the tips of his fingers.

Damir kicked off the wall and barreled into Simon's back. He turned midair and kicked Simon between the shoulders, propelling him just a little further. Pain shot through Simon like lightning from both blows, his vision blurring around the edges, but he was almost there.

Inches now, he reached again. Only seconds remained until the enemy ship could fire a shot into the helpless Persistence.

Simon's drift slowed and the wall approached painfully slowly. Damir struck the opposite wall at the far end of the Citadel.

Simon reached, extending his arm as far as it could go, and then a little further. He could see droplets of blood floating around him from his reopened wound.

His finger tapped the screen, and the green button changed from *Initiate* to *Executing...*

The camera feed showed a white-hot glow shortly before it went dead. The probe successfully injected thermite into the enemy cockpit, igniting everything and everyone within. The exterior metal began to melt, and the glass the probe had drilled through shattered in a violent explosion of sparks and fragments.

―――――

Simon held his side as he sat in the pilot's chair. "Have you found him yet?" he asked the control console.

"Yes, I see him just ahead," Damir responded from the radio in his environment suit. Simon rattled out a sigh of relief.

After the imminent threats were dispatched, Simon and Damir spent a painfully long time using the console in the Citadel to initiate an emergency lockdown of the Persistence. The emergency bulkhead sealed off the ship from space, and the primary cabin pressurized. With rudimentary control of the ship, they were able to correct the spin and reengage the artificial gravity.

The two left the Citadel once Simon found the controls among the options on the console and released the lock. Every loose item splayed out on the ground; it looked like a window was left open during a hurricane.

Simon wouldn't leave without Bill's body but was in no shape to go out for a spacewalk. Damir reluctantly agreed to find the pilot's corpse among the wreckage. He donned an environment suit from storage and braved the harsh expanse.

"I've got him," Damir relayed. "On my way back."

Simon wasn't ready to see Bill. He knew what happened to the human body when it was exposed to the vacuum of space, but the sight of Bill's bloated and icy skin haunted him. His frozen left arm had seemingly been struck by a piece of debris and was gone, shattered like glass.

Simon and Damir carried Bill to the Citadel and laid him on the bed that Simon had slept upon. He stared into Bill's red and lifeless eyes before covering him with a sheet.

"Do you know how to fly this?" Simon asked Damir in a low voice.

"I can get us to Harbor. This ship is different than what I'm used to, but I should be able to figure it out quickly enough."

Simon didn't look up from Bill as his eyes began welling with tears. "Good. Take us home."

"I also found this." Damir reached out and handed Simon a hat. *California Republic.* Simon grabbed it gently and stared at it. *The Persistence is yours, Simon.* Damir turned and left in silence.

Clutching the hat in one hand with the other resting on Bill's shoulder, Simon whispered, "Thank you, Bill."

SIMON CANSBY

Dreams came and went in the fever of recovery. Simon dreamt of home, both homes, in his stupor. He could feel his wound getting worse as time went on, his body aflame as it tried to fight off infection.

Simon dreamt of Harbor. Images of comradery amongst his peers as they began a new life together flashed intermittently. Rohan Avery scolded him, then laughed. Elder Munmer appeared from behind a corner to catch him and his friend attempting to pull a prank; it was, as Simon recounted, impossible to sneak around with a seer nearby. Elder Munmer smiled slightly as he walked away with a confiscated robotic bug that would hide and chime at random intervals.

Simon dreamt of Hemlock. His brothers looking for him as he hid in a tree. His mother cooking for him on his birthday, the light of the early evening star cut and interrupted by the mill before piercing the windows and bathing her in yellow. His father teaching him how to cut wood when he was young, the axe only a little too heavy for him.

Simon dreamt of Boe and wondered if she still thought of him as much as he continued to think of her.

"I've found something," Damir called over his shoulder to Simon as he flew the Persistence. Simon stirred, half awake and pale. He rose from his seat with a pained groan and hobbled to Damir. The *California Republic* hat lay perched atop the row of flight consoles.

"How far out are we?"

"Another hour and we'll be in range of Harbor's global positioning. Almost home."

Simon rasped out a sigh of weak relief. "What'd you find?"

"Here," Damir pointed to a display on his console board. "I was going through flight permissions when we passed through the trebuchet and I found this." On the screen were several columns of data, each line a recorded change. He tapped one row, and a page of information expanded. "A sub-registry. The Persistence is linked on a registry list for trebuchet permissions with a ship called the Progress."

Simon's face twisted in confusion. "That's weird. When did that happen?"

Damir surveyed the information. "The data starts on Argon. When did you guys go there?"

"Before I became a terrible Inquisitor. What kind of ship is it?"

"Just a sub-light freight carrier."

Simon began digging through his memory, searching for information, his brow rigid as he stared at the floor. *Where have I seen one of those lately?* He attempted to recall, but his mind was racked from the fever and likely concussed from recent conflicts. Simon was also distracted by the view of an ever-expanding Harbor through the window. He had never in his life felt more primed to sleep, like he could just drift where he stood.

"Let's just look into that later. I can't think right now."

———

The Persistence landed in the field of flowers. Several pages rushed to the landing pad, along with two elders and Rohan Avery, who were all prepared to receive Simon and treat his injuries. They stormed up the cargo ramp and laid him down on a gurney.

"Get him inside, now," Avery commanded. The pages wheeled him back to Temple Prime. He was asleep before they reached the doors.

In a haze, he drifted between consciousness and sleep over the following days. Simon was properly treated for his injuries by a medical scholar and his team of pages. They had received him just as an infection was setting in on the wound and a fever burned through him.

Occasionally, his peers would check in on him; Avery being the most common. He was surprised yet again by the seer, when Elder Munmer brought him water at the exact moment Simon was about to ask for it.

"How did you know?" Simon asked after Munmer entered the room and poured a glass of water from a carafe. He raised an eyebrow from behind a black blindfold; Simon *thought* he would be looking at him at that moment, but obviously couldn't be sure.

"It is truly astonishing, Simon, that, after all this time, my abilities still surprise you," he admitted with a smile. Simon drank greedily. After, he sat silently while Munmer checked bandages and nearby equipment. Before long, he thought of a question. "Being a seer doesn't mean I can see anything I want at any time," Munmer answered the question before it was asked. Simon stifled his surprise. "So, while I can get answers to some questions, most elude me. This is why we still need inquisitors. Sit up." Simon did as he was instructed and Munmer began to change the bandages around his side.

"Here's how it works," Munmer began, again starting just as Simon thought of the inquiry. "Most visions are sent to me haphazardly. It took many years of training to understand what I was seeing and even more to parse through the information for anything useful. This is how I knew you would need water and fresh bandages. There are also the larger visions that require a ritual. I can induce a trance through meditation and view things remotely."

Simon formed his lips into the beginning of another question. "I cannot, however," Munmer interrupted again, "view anything, anywhere at any time. There is an energy that is suffused in the galaxy that ebbs and flows like water. In some places, it is strong, in others, weak. It also changes as time passes. I am beholden to its will. Seers, like myself, have speculated that this energy is the presence of a Greater. It is not our place to know." Elder Munmer finished wrapping Simon's wound and helped lay him back down on the bed. He continued to stand near Simon silently, knowing something Simon didn't.

"Yes, I know what you're going to ask next," Munmer interjected, a grin starting to form on his face as Simon felt the faintest hint of frustration, "which is another reason why I've come here today. I performed a ritual last night, because I knew you wanted answers." Simon stared intently at the elder, but remained silent, knowing his curiosity would be sated. "I checked in on your family on Hemlock." Simon's heart began thumping against the boundary of his chest like it was trying to escape. "They are doing well, apart from your father, who is ill. Your mother and brother are worried about his health, but your brother has been taking care of the farm while your mother tends to your father. He will make a full recovery."

Simon released a breath so full of tension and anxiety it felt like it would come out as smoke and his eyes welled with tears of relief. Guilt washed over him as he hadn't thought of his family in some time. He assumed his brother had picked up the majority of the work around the farm and it was only then that he realized the scope of it. To handle the work normally catered to by five people, down to just three after Simon left, and now to one as his mother and father were waylaid, would require everything from him. All his free time, all the strength in his frame, spent.

Elder Munmer turned to leave just as the door opened. Avery stood behind it and held it open for the elder.

"Elder Munmer—" Simon began, hoping to catch him before he left.

"She is to be married soon," he informed as he stopped. "I'm sorry, Simon. Get some rest." *Come back to me.* He thought of the kiss she had left him with. It would likely be the last one. Munmer turned again and departed, leaving Avery in the doorframe.

"How are you doing?" Avery asked with a perceptive look.

"I have no idea."

Avery closed the door. "Understandable. I wanted to say just how proud of you I am." He sat on a nearby chair. "The first paladin to fight a real AI in hundreds of years and you came out in one piece. Incredible."

"Thank you, Rohan." Simon's pride glowed for a moment but was snuffed out by the news he'd received moments ago. Then, a realization. "Wait, how did you know about that? I've been in here for almost a week and nobody's come to debrief me. After everything I said about the emperor, I figured everyone would be clamoring for answers."

Avery dipped his head and sighed. "Stories have circulated since you've been down. Hailey Svarthold has taken her throne and sent news of a conspiracy between the Core worlds and the emperor. The information we were looking for regarding Sir Alan Harbrand was delivered to the Core fleets via an agent among Hailey's ranks. Now discourse is brewing among great houses. A few are rallying behind Hailey's banner. The whole situation isn't looking good."

"So, Harbrand is exonerated, then?"

"He would be, if he hadn't fled Harbor."

"*He fled?!*"

"He fled. We're trying to discern to where, but the investigation is still ongoing."

"Are you kidding me?!" Simon's volume elevated. "I didn't have to go on this mission at all and to top it off, the Order couldn't detain ONE MAN?!" Simon's side began to pulse in pain as he yelled.

"Ok, you're right to be upset about Harbrand, but we were all *extremely* lucky you were there. Taking down that AI drone was the most important thing you could have done on that mission."

"What about Damir's information? The emperor commissioned incredibly illegal surveillance of a great house. Imperial ships killed thousands of Karakura sailors, including some of their nobility. What's to be done?"

Avery dipped his head again. "I'm not sure anything will be done."

Simon stared daggers at him. "*What?*"

"It seems like there is some evidence against our elders that imperial intelligence has a hold of. The council is saying that we can't take sides in this conflict, but I feel that's just a cover."

"There are no sides in this conflict."

"There are, Simon. Hailey is alive because of illegal technology, wandering about in a metal body. No matter which side the Order takes, we'd be supporting the use of outlawed technology."

"Well, if that's the case, then it's a zero-sum game and we should oppose the side that *murdered innocent* Karakura sailors and conspired to steal an entire sector of the galaxy!"

"It's not that simple, Simon."

"It is *that simple!* Tell me the oath you took."

"I'm not going to—"

"'I will be a willing agent, protecting mankind from threats *within* and without.' We took an oath, Rohan. Adhere to it."

"What do you want me to do?" Avery stood suddenly, his frustration beginning to boil over in synchrony with Simon's. "We are obliged to the council and its orders, despite our oaths. We can't just start swinging."

Simon breathed heavily through the pain in his side. Both paladins went silent for a moment, allowing the heat to dissipate between them.

"So you're not happy with their decisions, either?" Simon asked.

"Of course not. But what can we do?"

What can we do? Simon thought. *We can't take on an entire empire.* Simon turned the options over in his mind. Either concede and follow blindly along with what the Order and the council deems is right, forsaking the truth in his oath, or act on what his heart tells him is right and do something that will label him an oath breaker.

Give up or give everything up.

What can we do?

HAILEY SVARTHOLD

She allowed herself some room to pace. After speaking with her constituents, as the sound of fighting grew ever louder, she somehow grew to understand Henry's disdain of the throne itself. Never would she have guessed that she would align with him in so small a matter while her world burned around her.

Hailey walked left to right in front of the throne wrought of marble while Sir Gerard and Alister Brightwater advised her on the status of the front, a large wooden table standing between them and the door. Kenji had recovered enough to be mobile and attended these meetings, though he didn't have much he wanted to contribute.

"How long do we have?" Hailey asked, pacing left.

"Days, if we're lucky," Alister answered stoically.

"How about civilians? Are there any left in the city?"

"As per my most recent reports," Gerard apprised, "the majority of the population of Nymeria has vacated through the southern and western gates and are in temporary shelters set up in the towns of Larsden and West Lake. We have a representative from West Lake here today that was hoping to speak with you."

"In person?" Hailey asked, shocked.

"Aye, my lady. I can summon him if you'd like."

"Please do. Thank you, Gerry."

Gerard bowed and left the throne room. Hailey continued to walk a hole in the ground in front of her throne. A façade of cool composure was the only thing keeping the flood of distress and worry at bay. *If only I could take a deep breath.*

Gerard returned with a man dressed in a black suit still wrinkled from the bag he assumedly removed it from a short time before the meeting. He was escorted into the room and around the dark wood table. "Lady Hailey Svarthold, Lord and Protector of the Outer Reach and Arcturus," Gerard heralded. The man stepped forward, slightly timid, and bowed. "Sheriff Emerson of West Lake presents himself to the court, my lady."

I didn't think I'd be sick of being called lady so quickly, Hailey thought, annoyed at the grandiose procedure.

"Thank you, Sherriff Emerson, for travelling here to the capital during wartime. I understand that it can't have been easy. Please, tell me why you've come," she requested, pacing right.

"My lady Svarthold, West Lake has received a great number of refugees from Nymeria," Emerson began nervously. "Circumstances are dire, I understand, but we are already running dangerously low on food and medical supplies. We need your help. My lady."

"There's no need for the honorifics," Hailey decided bluntly after Emerson hastily appended one to his request. It seemed like everyone was uncertain on which title to use, Lord or Lady, as it wasn't common to have female nobility. "We're past that point in this meeting. The refugees have depleted your town's supplies, what's happened to the distribution from the farmlands to the northwest?"

"Primary distribution is staged out of Nymeria, my lady," Gerard interjected. "All supply lines from the farmlands are brought here first and distributed."

"That's correct," Emerson continued. "With the war, food just isn't being delivered. That's only one part of the issue, however. A large portion of our food and all medical supplies are manufactured off-world. Obviously, the Core fleets aren't letting any new supplies in. We need relief or there may be hoarding, which will likely turn to violence."

Hailey's first dilemma as leader. The war was obligatory and simple; mitigate damage, keep her people from being killed. Keeping people fed and healthy was an entirely different beast in need of taming.

She stopped pacing.

"Do you have anywhere in West Lake that would allow for proper storage of food?" Hailey inquired analytically.

"I think so. There is an arts building with an auditorium. We should be able to convert it into temporary storage."

"Good. I'll send word to the Edelin Farms to continue distribution but divert it to West Lake. You'll assess and split the product with Larsden. This should hold us over until we can get trade re-established."

"Thank you, my lady, but that could take weeks. We don't have that long."

Hailey looked to Gerard. "Distribution was staged out of Nymeria, right? Are any of the warehouses accessible?"

He lifted his tablet and tapped on it for a few moments. "Two are within the hot zone. There was one more that burnt down, but it looks like there might be one north of here that may still have supplies. It is in the manufacturing district, which was one of the first parts of town to empty out and has remained relatively untouched."

"Secure that warehouse and its supplies. Divert men away from palace security if need be." She turned back to Emerson. "Please stay here in the meantime. I would like you to return home with the food. Remind my people that their liege lord will not let them wither."

"Thank you, my lady." Emerson bowed and took his leave.

The throne room fell silent after the doors closed, apart from the booms and cracks of war, the palace walls simultaneously muffling and amplifying them like a drum. The sounds had been getting louder for days.

"My lady," Alister began, "I fear we don't have long until the Blackhats will have taken the palace. My men are stretched thin, and with the entirety of the Core fleets in orbit, it doesn't seem like their ranks are going to deplete any time soon. If we could—" Alister broke off and held his hand to his ear, listening intently. "Something's happening, they've made a violent push. My men are retreating," he informed in a panic. "They're not sure what's caused it, but the Blackhats are reckless."

"How long do we have?" Hailey demanded.

Alister listened in silence, hand to his ear. Suddenly, his eyes darted up in alarm. "My lady, we nee—"

A lateral rainstorm of shattered glass behind a deafening explosion threw everyone to the ground. The tall windows had blown out from the concussion of several Blackhat drop pods hitting the walls and roof of the palace in quick succession.

Hailey rolled as she hit the floor, her frame clanking as it made impact. Glass ground beneath her weight against the marble, crackling as it turned to dust. She lifted her head and met Kenji's stunned gaze; prone and bleeding from a cut on the head, he lay a few feet away. Alister laid motionless a few feet further off to her left. Gerard had already begun to lift himself from the floor.

"Hailey!" he screamed, scanning the room.

"Gerry!" she replied as she stood. "I'm here, check on Alister!" Gerard nodded and limped to Alister. Hailey picked up Kenji.

"Are you ok?" she asked in a hurry.

"I'll be fine," he answered breathily, shaking off a daze.

"We have to get out of here. Now." Hailey started for the door, but Kenji wasn't following. She turned back, "Kenji!" she screamed. "Let's go!"

Three men in gloss black armor stormed through the blown open throne room doors holding rifles. Moving like shadows, they acquired their targets, Gerard and Alister, and aimed their weapons. Gerard was still lifting Alister from the floor when he spotted the trio. All too late, he stared at them with wide eyes.

Hailey ran forward and kicked the table. With the immense, inhuman strength in her frame, it slid across the stone floor with violent speed, screeching as it soared. The table crashed into the soldiers and flipped as it hit. The three men reeled from the impact and were sent backward in a tumble, their weapons thrown from their hands.

A low, percussive thrum pierced the air and drew Hailey's attention to the windows.

"They're cornered!" screamed Kenji. "They're pushing the attack because they're surrounded!"

In the sky, she saw salvation. Through the haze of dust, through the smoke of Nymeria burning, through the clouds painted orange, she saw it. Her bannermen.

KENJI KARAKURA

Kenji lifted his hand to his head then retracted it, noticing the blood on his fingers. Whether it was the light-headed daze, or the wondrous sight of friendly ships in orbit, he couldn't be sure, but he felt no fear at that moment. He limped forward, the pain in his ribs only a mild suggestion.

Motionless, Hailey stood in the obliterated throne room and stared out the windows. Kenji stopped to stand at her side and the two of them witnessed an orbital battle; history taking shape in front of them.

Four flagships followed by dozens of corvettes and hundreds of single-pilot fighters pressed their attack against the fleets of the Core. Salvos of shots raked against the Peregrin from two of the leading flagships. Four corvettes swooped underneath and began peppering the shields of its underbelly, swarming the Blackhat battleship, the Enfilade, after they passed the Peregrin.

The Peregrin began a counterattack and unloaded shots against the forward-most flagship while its bay doors opened, unleashing a cloud of Kestrels.

"Gerard!" Hailey turned and screamed. "Get your men down to Harvest Point! I want our fleet in the air yesterday!"

"My lady," he said softly. Kenji turned away from the windows to notice Gerard kneeling down with Alister, who had been shot. Still taking in ragged breaths, he held his hand over his blood covered side. "They got a shot off before the table hit them."

Hailey rushed to their side. "Go," she commanded, "I'll get him some help."

"I'll not leave my ward while our home is being assailed," Gerard announced in defiance.

Hailey snapped a look at Gerard, but Alister interrupted. "You get your ass down there," he coughed. "My men better not have died for no reason. Get that fucking fleet in the air and push them back. Your lord commands it."

Gerard stood fast; defiance born of loyalty.

"I'll go," Kenji volunteered. "I am an admiral, after all. I'll get your fleet airborne, and we'll push these bastards back."

Hailey nodded at Kenji. "There are tunnels that lead to Harvest Point, that's the bay where the fleet is stored. The entrance to the tunnel is under the library. Sailors aboard the ships have been waiting for an opportunity to launch."

"Standby crews," Gerard informed. "The numbers on board are slim, but there should be enough men to get the job done. Find the boathouse with the Svarthold emblem on the door."

"Go, Kenji," Hailey pleaded. "Help me get my home back."

Kenji nodded and ran out the doors.

In the panic of the assault, Kenji found Takeshi, wandering aimlessly in shock around the halls of the palace. Kenji grabbed him by the shirt and commanded him to follow.

They heard more pods crack into the ground just outside the walls as Kenji found the tunnel entrance in the library; the sound of impact deadened through the white stone.

A false wall opened in the bookshelves and a dark passage unfurled in front of them. Kenji took no time, had no patience for caution, and he pressed forward into the gloom.

With the light on his tablet, he marched through the featureless tunnel toward Harvest Point. Occasionally looking behind him to see Takeshi following with terror in his eyes.

The tunnel bore straight for a few hundred meters, before it curved left and opened into a cavern. The ceiling was half natural, half carved. In the center was a freight car sitting on mag-lev rails, the rails continuing into a narrow tunnel to his right, further into the dark.

Kenji surmised that this was an escape route for the people of the palace, allowing for quick withdrawal to the fleets in case of attack. Given how long the Svartholds had lived in peace, he guessed that the rail car was older than he was and likely hadn't been used for a long time. Kenji hoped it worked.

He found an access panel near the parked rail car and clicked a switch into the *on* position. The cavern bloomed in fluorescent light as everything came to life; the overhead lights bathed the railcar in a blueish white hue, and they continued to click on in quick sequence down the mag-lev tunnel.

A screen on the access panel flickered on and displayed a few options. Kenji found the *activate* option, then the button for *Harvest Point*. The doors on the freight car slid open as the screen displayed text asking the controller to *please board...*

The freight car had two rows of seats and an empty area in the rear for storage. At the front of the car sat another control panel. The screen read *depart* on a bright green prompt.

Kenji almost sat down when he noticed Takeshi standing outside the car, staring at the surrounding cavern, frozen in fear.

"Takeshi," Kenji began softly, "we need to go."

"I can't," Takeshi said as he started to shake his head. "More soldiers will be down there, Kenji. Please, I can't." His breathing increased in frequency as his eyes filled with tears. "You said we weren't made for this, Kenji. We're going back into a ship and headed straight for a battle in orbit. I'm not made for this, Kenji!"

Kenji stepped out of the rail car and approached Takeshi. He lifted his hand and set it gently on Takeshi's shoulder. "Tak," he continued in his soft timbre, "we aren't made for this. Everything we've been through has been a trial meant to break us; meant to take all we have. But we're still here. You asked me how do we do it? How do we be brave? It is exactly in this moment, when your brain is screaming at you to run, when your nerves are on fire from adrenaline. It is only in moments like this that we can be brave. Hailey needs you, Tak. The people of Nymeria need you. *I need you.*"

Minutes later, they barreled through the featureless tunnel in the freight car, away from the palace toward Harvest Point; toward the submerged Svarthold fleet that would be Hailey's lifeline. Kenji stared forward through the glass, watching hundreds of lights pass above at immense speed. The smooth walls blurred and started to look like he was in a trebuchet throw, traveling well beyond the speed of light.

Before long, an exit point appeared and grew, the light of day getting brighter as the freight car sped closer. Kenji felt a lurch as the car decelerated out of the tunnel. One hundred meters of open ground separated Kenji from the coastal buildings at Harvest Point. The freight car slowed to a stop at the end of the line, the mag-lev rails cutting off abruptly.

Kenji's eyes adjusted to the light pouring in through the windows. Around him lay a no-mans-land of scarred ground and rubble, the streets pockmarked with craters from munitions. The Core fleets pushed their attack, flexing the defenses around Nymeria to a breaking point.

Two drop pods crashed into the ground ahead of the freight car with a thunderous crack, throwing debris and dust indiscriminately. Kenji took cover behind the panels of the car as gunfire pelted it, shattering the windows above him.

One hundred meters, he thought, *can we make it if we make a break for it? I didn't see any cover. I don't have a weapon to return fire.* He attempted to find a solution to an impossible problem as brutality tore at the metal panels against his back. A hole in the car appeared next to his head as a projectile sheered through. *We can't die here!*

A reflection of light shined in his eyes, and he looked up to find the source. A ship had entered the atmosphere, focusing the light of the Arcturan star from reflective metal panels. It hovered above the city menacingly. The new ship was long and rectangular, with portholes lining the bottom from bow to stern. This wasn't a traditional fleet ship, not a corvette or freight carrier or gunship. It was familiar to Kenji.

With rapid sequential explosions, it began firing from the portholes, back to front. The projectiles slowed in the air, too large to be munitions. *Breach pods.*

Karakura Breach Pods.

A Karakura Drop Ship had joined the fray and peppered the ground with reinforcements. The ground shook like it was being hit with a drum roll as the pods struck Arcturus.

Kenji noticed the enemy fire against his back had stopped. He dared to peek above his cover just as a breach pod landed in front of him. Out poured four Karakura soldiers, rifles raised to return fire. One of the soldiers stepped ahead of the others and slammed a spike in the ground. The spike deployed and a metal wall expanded, giving the soldiers cover from the enemy fire.

"Takeshi!" Kenji screamed in elation. He looked down to his friend who had taken cover next to him, still frozen with his back against the car door. "Karakuras! They're here!"

Kenji kicked the car door open and grabbed Takeshi. The two braved the dusty expanse, ducking their heads as they ran. They crossed the barren swathe screaming, "Friendly! Karakura!" as they approached their kinsmen. A soldier broke away from cover and returned fire to the Blackhats as Kenji and Takeshi grew nearer. "Suppress fire!" he ordered.

Kenji threw himself to the ground behind the temporary wall, Takeshi falling nearby. The soldier that broke away returned and ducked, meeting Kenji on the ground.

"I am Kenji Karakura!" he announced above the cacophony surrounding them. "Rear Admiral of the Fifth Fleet! Get me to those buildings!" he commanded as he pointed to the Harvest Point shoreline. The trooper's face hid behind an armored atmosphere helmet, black tinted glass set within glossy, dark blue armor plating. He returned, what Kenji could only guess was a stoic stare. Kenji lifted himself to a crouch. "I am your admiral! Get me to those buildings!" The soldier looked to his fellow men, all returning a silent stare awaiting command.

The commander issued a curt nod, and the squad sprang into action. Three stood and began firing at their assailants. The fourth tapped commands into the tablet on his wrist. The chest-high wall deployed panels out of its base; one on each side. The front panel extended forward and dug into the ground; the rear dug in next to the wall. The new panels acted as a base as the wall lifted and slid forward along rails. At the end of the track, the wall lowered and planted itself, allowing the panels to reposition and repeat the process, moving the cover forward in a crawl.

Kenji kept his head low and moved with the group, keeping an eye on Takeshi, who had reluctantly joined him in this endeavor. Fire crackled over their heads as they progressed. He was grossly proud of these fighters at this moment; they were efficient, quick and brutal. As the leader issued commands, the rest followed with robotic swiftness. Whenever one ducked to reload, another would pop up to cover the hole they left, creating a storm of ever encroaching bombardment.

After five minutes of deafening combat, the sound washed into ringing in Kenji's ears. He looked up to see all the men had stopped fighting, the commander ushering him toward the buildings, screaming to get up and move.

Kenji did as he was told and lifted himself and Takeshi to begin the run forward. Surrounded by a phalanx of Karakura fighters, they passed six Blackhat soldiers dead on the ground. Through haze and dust, they marched forward to the few lone buildings along the shore.

Harvest Point was, ostensibly, a simple port that brought in trade goods to Nymeria from nearby coastal towns. The port had hidden the secret of Arcturus's firepower for so long, most had forgotten that the Svartholds had a fleet at all.

They reached a boat house at the end of a long pier that hung out above the water. Kenji pointed at the door emblazoned with the Svarthold house emblem and one from the squad rushed forward to kick it open. The team cleared the building quickly and signaled Kenji to follow.

The boat house was almost entirely empty aside from the industrial elevator near the water. It was large enough to carry pallets of supplies and groups of sailors down to the awaiting ships below the swell.

Kenji hailed the elevator and turned to the squad that had escorted them while it ascended. "Thank you. You all fought well today."

The commander nodded to Kenji, "You honor us, my lord. It is a blessing; we were ordered to push back the Core fleets and assist the Svartholds in this siege, but as a secondary objective, we were instructed to find you. Lord Karakura wants to ensure your safety in this battle."

"Chiyo said that?" Kenji choked.

"Aye, Lord Chiyo Karakura has been very concerned with your welfare. My squad and I are incredibly honored to fight for you."

"That's extremely lucky, how did you know where I'd be?"

"I misspoke. Every soldier aboard that drop ship was told to find you. My men and I are the lucky ones."

Kenji stood dumbfounded as Takeshi set a gentle hand on his shoulder. There, in the middle of a warzone, he thought of his father. He thought of his mother. He thought of Clara. *I'm not a coward,* he told himself, *and I'm not done.*

The elevator dinged and the doors hissed open.

"Everyone in."

HAILEY SVARTHOLD

Just a little longer, she reassured herself as the doors to the library were battered. *The Pteron will be out of the water soon.* She looked around; barricaded in the library with her were five of the Svarthold house guard, Sir Gerard, and Captain Alister Brightwater, who was slumped against a wall, barely holding onto consciousness while he held onto a pistol.

The door bowed from the force of another blow. *I won't let it be for nothing.* She had never held a rifle before. She stood behind her men, with Gerard at her side, weapon trained on the entrance. She couldn't fathom why so many had placed their loyalty in her, couldn't believe the path she had been on thus far, but she knew she needed to be what her father couldn't: a leader.

Death knocked on the door again and the sound boomed through a squad of silent sentinels. Hailey heard the breath of the men as they stared intensely at the barricaded double doors. She heard more drop pods pummeling the ground. She heard men dying nearby, muffled by the white marble. She heard footfalls as troops trampled through her home, through her family's memories.

Another boom preceded a nauseating crack. The door was weakening; its supports giving way underneath the pressure. *If I survive this, no enemy boots will ever land on my planet again,* she vowed, sending her missive to the stars in the hope that they took note.

A few errant splinters shot forward as they struck the door once more.

"One more and they're through," Gerard whispered to them. "Fire at anything that comes through that door."

One more. She tensed, the strength of her hand warping the grip of the rifle. *Fire at anything.* Hailey had never killed anyone before today. She wasn't sure if the men that had been hit by the speeding table were dead. Breath held, as far as she could tell, the room seemed to freeze in anticipation.

One of the men exhaled, he couldn't hold his breath any longer, his weapon shook in his hand. Another looked to the soldier to his right. Gerard coughed faintly. They all waited.

And waited.

The silence broke as rifle fire sounded off on the other side of the door. Hailey jumped with a start, her weapon trained at the door. Her grip on the rifle was so tight that the grip snapped off in her hand.

Through the door, she could hear clashing and firearms blasting from different points beyond the wall in front of them. The men surrounding her looked to each other in verification, to be sure they were all experiencing the same event. She could hear men dying. Some yelled orders, muted by the stone around them. Boots clacked against the hard floors as weapons screamed from opposing sides.

As swiftly as it had left, silence returned.

Hailey heard breathing among her house guard as they shifted their feet nervously, weapons continuously focused on the door.

Hailey and her men spent an agonizing pause before a rapping sounded at the door. A simple knock, like a friend had arrived unexpectedly.

"This is Major Hitori Karakura," a deadened voice spoke through the door, "of the Karakura Navy. We've dispatched the Blackhats attempting to break in."

Gerard held a finger to his lips, silently ordering everybody in the room to remain quiet. They waited, unsure if they were being tricked.

"Find Hailey Svarthold," the voice through the door continued, facing away. "Secure the palace and find Kenji Karakura. Lord Chiyo needs a report on his status." She heard the footfalls head away from the library.

Hailey lowered her weapon, feeling like her eyes would be wide in this moment. "HERE!" she shouted in delayed response.

"My lady!" Gerard whispered.

"How would they know about Kenji? As far as the Core fleets know, the Karakuras had already been taken off the board. Stand down." She passed alongside her men and stepped closer to the door. "Hitori, are you there?"

"Aye!" he shouted.

"This is Hailey Svarthold. Thank you for your timely arrival."

"The honor is mine, Lady Svarthold. Are you injured?"

"I'm fine. We'll be out in a minute; we need to take down these barricades." Hailey's vision darkened and she whipped her head to the library window. Elated and relieved, she saw a leviathan rise from the northeast, blotting the sun as it ascended.

"Have you seen Lord Kenji Karakura?" he asked. "Is he safe? Do you know where he is?"

She felt laughter in her chest. Somehow, impossibly, she felt lightheaded. "He's aboard the Pteron."

KENJI KARAKURA

Kenji grabbed the railing as the Pteron jerked to one side, its propulsion systems still waking up. It hiccupped and sputtered.

"I need a sitrep, now," he ordered from the elevated command platform.

"Backblow from the engines, my lord," a Svarthold soldier informed him from a station to his left. "This is normally an issue we bypass with more warmup time."

"Your recommendations on warmup time have been noted." The angle of the Pteron began to right itself and Kenji's iron grip on the railing loosened. "I need to know if it's going to stay in the air."

"Aye, my Lord."

"Communications - status of the other ships in the fleet." Water rushed off the front window of the bridge as the ship climbed.

"Fleet at eighty-four percent strength. Projections show that number will increase to ninety-one once the corvettes have had some time to boot up."

"It will have to do. Set vector and begin climb. Divert power from non-essential systems," he issued to navigation before turning to communications. "Open a wideband to the fleet."

The communications officer tapped away on her keyboard for a moment. "Wideband is live."

"This is Admiral Kenji Karakura. I have been ordered by Lady Svarthold to take control of your Navy. Your bannermen are fighting a battle above us that they cannot win. They have taken oaths, much like all of you, and are bravely fulfilling them, but they face a force that will overwhelm them. This is why we fly with cold engines. We are joining that fight to fulfil our oaths.

"I know there aren't many of you still aboard these ships, but it will not matter. I know these ships haven't flown in years, but it will not matter. I know you are all as scared as I am, but it will not matter. These problems will seem inconsequential because by the end of the day, you will have forced the enemy back. By the end of this battle, you will have driven these oppressors from your home. By the end of your life, you will remember this day with fondness, knowing you bravely fought to defend your home with friends at your side. Onward, kinsmen, to battle stations!"

The line went dead at the flick of a switch. Every eye was upon Kenji at that moment, with only the rough hum of the engines and his heartbeat in his ears.

The squad of armored Karakura soldiers removed their helmets and bowed. The communications officer stood and saluted, as did the navigations officer, as did the systems officer. Takeshi Yamada smiled at his friend.

Kenji stood in reverence of the people that surrounded him. Pride bloomed in his heart at the thought of commanding the battleship that had once saved his people. *If the only way my life has any meaning is through my death, then let it be this death.*

The Pteron forged a path through the sky as it ascended to join the fray above, its engines burning hot as it climbed. Kenji saw Nymeria as above it, a Karakura drop ship hovered. Smoke rose in columns dotted across the city, but amongst the immense destruction, he couldn't help but notice that the city shone like a jewel.

They ripped through the atmosphere in force. Alongside the Pteron were four corvettes and a flagship, and peppered between were dozens of Valari; single-pilot fighters. Another sub-battleship and five more corvettes trailed as they attempted to catch up to the rest of the fleet.

The rumbling from the atmospheric resistance disappeared instantly as they breached into space. Ahead of them lay ruination; fragments of shattered ships reflected the sunlight intermittently, explosions painted the scene with a discomforting hush, munitions flew like animated dotted lines.

"Draw up to their port flank, ready guns on starboard side." Kenji issued orders as the fleet approached.

The Kopesh flagship, the Nefertum, received a major blow to its shields from the Peregrin and was reeling, opening its side to further attacks from Kestrels as it attempted to change direction.

"Valari to intercept Kestrels, assist the Nefertum with retreat." A cloud tore past the Pteron and suffused with the battle, setting Kenji's view alight as the single-man fighters met the enemy. The Nefertum corrected its trajectory to get out of direct fire from the Peregrin and the Forgeman flagship, the Hyacinth, filled the gap.

With three flagships raking its port flank, the Peregrin stood as a barrier for the Arbir, the Harbrand battleship, to return fire to the Svarthold bannermen. The Arbir attempted to crest above the Peregrin. The Enfilade, the Blackhat battleship, attempted to fight back against the rest of the Forgeman corvettes that had passed below the Peregrin.

"All power forward, intercept Peregrin's trajectory and flank the Arbir." The Pteron raced forward to align itself perpendicular to the enemy ships. After passing the Peregrin, it turned to open its starboard flank to the Arbir.

"Starboard guns," Kenji commanded as his hands shook. "Fire!"

A hail of Svarthold rage bloomed from the Pteron and raked the Arbir as it attempted its maneuver. The Arbir turned as it ascended, its top-mounted turret twisted to target the Pteron.

"BRACE!"

A shot from the turret pummeled into the Pteron and Kenji's footing wavered as the floor shook underneath him. Alarm sirens sounded on the bridge. The projectile tore a hole in the ship's shields and its armor.

"Seal off breached compartments," Kenji directed as his officers scrambled. "Adjust trajectory 45 degrees starboard." The Pteron turned and positioned itself just as the Arbir fired another round. The shot glanced off the shields and was sent barrelling into space. Kenji poured over a holographic readout of the battle. "Corvettes four, five, thirteen and twenty-one, set course for the Arbir and take that gun out. We'll open a hole."

The Hyacinth received a blow from the Peregrin, knocking out its shields. After the blow had been dealt, the Forgeman flagship was defenseless. Kenji noticed a sudden divergence of trajectory and the Hyacinth pressed forward at maximum speed to ram the Peregrin.

It collided with the port side of the Peregrin, their shields not designed to stop a projectile that large. Sparks erupted from the point of impact. The Peregrin began to list to starboard, while the Hyacinth snapped apart in four places. Escape pods broke away and dispersed, aiming for Arcturus.

Admiral Robert Forgeman sounded off from Kenji's communications terminal on a wideband to the entire fleet. "My crew have cleared the ship! The Hyacinth is stuck and interrupting the Peregrin's shields from reforming around it! FIRE ON MY POSITION! FIRE INTO THE HYACINTH!"

Four corvettes pressured the Arbir as the Peregrin listed into its path. "Fire on the Arbir," Kenji commanded. "Clear its shields." The starboard guns blasted, and their projectiles landed on the Arbir, tearing a hole in its shields. The corvettes swooped by and raked fire along its barren top, ripping through the top-mounted cannon.

The Hill flagship, the Inverness, pushed forward and aligned with the Hyacinth, aiming its primary forward railgun straight down the length of the Forgeman flagship embedded in the Peregrin. The Brightwater flagship, the Coyote, followed suit and closed the gap. Positioned beneath the Inverness, it aimed its starboard cannons at the Hyacinth.

The two titans fired their perspective weapons at the wreckage lodged into the side of the Peregrin. The Coyote went first; it unleashed a barrage that cracked through the destroyed remnants, sheering off panels and columns inside the ship. Inverness' forward railgun glowed white hot at the tip and, with ominous silence, unleashed a single projectile into and through the Hyacinth; it pierced the exterior of the Peregrin and shredded everything in its path until it came out the other side. The railgun's shot bounced off the inside of the Peregrin's starboard side shields and deflected back into the ship. It ricocheted three more times, each time grabbing chunks of the Peregrin as it passed, until it stopped, lodged in the Glasser flagship's engines.

Sporadically, explosions popped down the length of the Peregrin from its interior. Escape pods fired out the sides in long sequences.

"Send a message down to Nymeria Command. Tell them the Peregrin has been disabled, and to be on the lookout for Glasser escape pods on the surface." Kenji issued the command as he turned his attention from the escape pods to the wreckage of the Hyacinth. It smoldered white hot as pieces flew away, until it crumbled completely, adding to the cloud of debris surrounding them.

"Thank you, Forgeman," Kenji said under his breath, acknowledging the captain that went down with his ship.

———

A few miles from Nymeria, the Pteron landed after the battle, along with the smoking hulks of the Coyote, Nefertum and Inverness, on a farm among its crops. Kenji looked upon them with wonder; the towering leviathans that he knew would become as famous as the Pteron.

Before long, the respective admirals joined him as they waited for pickup. He, Jerome Brightwater, Harriot Kopesh, and Rickard Hill didn't say a word as they reflected. The wind picked up and sang a hushed song, extracting the anxiety that had embedded itself within Kenji.

After the Peregrin had been destroyed, the remaining fleets retreated, with only the occasional errant straggler left behind. In total, five corvettes and seventeen single-pilot fighters surrendered and were captured. Fifty-seven escape pods were also seized, and their passengers arrested.

Kenji had been floating in a daze since their victory. He remembered with the clarity of a dream that his officers cheered as they drove the enemy back. He stood beside himself, truly uncertain if anything he saw was real; a feeling made stronger by the scale of the ships he stood before.

A familiar face popped out from behind the gargantuan landing equipment and rushed to them, throwing his arms around Kenji. With a wide grin, David Hill released him from the hug and patted him on the back.

You've done very well, Kenji. An image of his uncle bestowing on him the honor of rear admiral.

Kenji felt the message from the little Carthian as he made his presence known. Kenji smiled. *Thank you,* he thought in response, *I was needed here.*

The three spent their ride back to the palace filling each other in on the events they had each experienced. David had had a colorful journey, wherein he was almost apprehended by the Falconers as a traitor. Kenji surmised that David's apprehension about asking for their help was justified. David had also sent word to the Karakuras that Kenji was still alive. He didn't hear any correspondence after that message and wasn't sure they were going to do anything.

Kenji was beyond thankful; he just didn't know how to express it. He felt like a ghost, disassociated from the world, but forced to watch and listen.

The admirals arrived back at the palace and were received with roaring applause. Every soldier and commander of the Svarthold Army, Navy and house guard that remained waited for the heroes of the Siege of Arcturus.

A crowd surrounded them as the panel door to their cab opened to the courtyard in front of the palace door. Wreckage and detritus surrounded them as they shuffled out of the cab and into the waiting arms of the enraptured horde. Smiles curled upward to meet the edges of tired eyes; applause and shouts seemed to melt into a single continuous noise.

Kenji jumped at the sound of a champagne cork being popped, followed by another. He looked around to see that the palace stores were raided for the celebration; barrels and bottles were carried inside among the throng.

Through the scorched halls, the admirals were shepherded. Chants rang down the white walls and echoed off the pockmarked floors.

They turned a corner to see the throne room with broken glass covering the ground, and a chunk taken out of the throne itself. This didn't dampen anyone's spirits, as the crowd poured in through the door and filled the space, glass crunching under their feet.

Hailey stood before her throne with her arms behind her. Sir Gerard stood at her side beaming, dried blood still caked on his head.

"Admirals!" Hailey announced over the tumult of voices. It took a few moments for the volume to reduce enough for her to speak. Kenji noticed some of the troops and captains looking at Hailey with surprise, her metallic form a strange sight. "Admirals," she continued, "you have proven yourselves to be the embodiment of bravery and loyalty today. I cannot begin to describe how grateful I am that, when called, you did not hesitate to answer." Hailey stepped forward and down from the dais. She noticed David and paused, then turned to his father. "Lord Hill, I imagine you are very proud of your son," she stated to Admiral Rickard Hill.

"My Lady, thank you, I am," he responded timidly with a bow.

"A Hill knows where his honor lies," she said, and Rickard's eyes perked up, "and I can assure you that a Svarthold does as well." He flashed a smile that was brimming with pride toward his son.

"I understand that we lost an admiral," she continued.

"Admiral Robert Forgeman," Kenji recounted. "He opened up the defenses of the Peregrin and went down with his ship."

Hailey dipped her head and remained silent for a moment. "I see. I don't know what to say." She began to pace slowly. "I will see that he receives posthumous honors, the highest I can bestow. Even that feels cheap in comparison to what he's given me... All I can say is *thank you.*" She turned and faced more of the general crowd. "Thank you to everyone who put your lives on the line today. Let's take a moment and have a drink in celebration."

The throne room was electric with a cheerful hum as the victorious poured wine, beer and champagne into whatever they could find that would hold liquid. Kenji even saw a soldier decant a bottle of wine into his hat, sipping as his friends laughed.

Kenji shook more hands than he could count; never before had he felt like a celebrity, even as nephew of the Lord of the Inner Reach. During the commotion, he caught the eye of Takeshi, who looked on and smiled. Kenji smiled back, happy to have his friend to anchor him to the moment. He walked beside him, almost autonomously.

Hailey was seen reassuring Jerome Brightwater that Alister was recovering in the hospital. After he thanked her and left, she approached Kenji. "What'd I tell you?" she asked with a smile in her voice. Kenji cocked his head to the side with feigned ignorance and grinned. "I *told you* your family would see you as a hero." Kenji looked to the floor out of modesty. Hailey leaned forward and quietly said, "I couldn't have done this without you, Kenji. Thank you." She placed a hand on his shoulder. Kenji placed his hand on hers and they took a moment to appreciate each other.

Her hand locked and became rigid, starting to hurt Kenji.

"Ok, I get it!" he said with a laugh. His smile soured as she stood frozen. "Hailey?"

She collapsed in front of him, crumpling into a metal heap on the floor. He tried to catch her, but Hailey's robotic frame was too heavy, and he fell with her. The series of clangs drew the attention of many around them and they grew quiet. Gerard rushed over and fell to his knees around her.

"What happened?!" he screamed.

"I- I don't know," Kenji stuttered, "I just- we were talking and she went quiet. I don't know."

David pushed his way through the crowd. "What happened?"

"I don't know!" Kenji screamed in frustration. "She just went quiet and collapsed!"

David's face went dark. "Oh no," he whispered.

"What is it?" Gerard asked hurriedly.

"Her... her engram. It's still decaying."

HAILEY SVARTHOLD

-Initialize

EPILOGUE

EDGAR THRAWL

The grey stone sapped the heat from the room. Edgar sat huddled in his blanket on a cot in the corner of his cell, determined to hold onto whatever warmth he had left.

His arm throbbed. The stump where his arm used to be, was an incessant reminder of his failure. The pages had been diligent, at the very least, and the glaive that took his limb was impossibly sharp, so the wound was healing well. His heart, however, would never heal.

Dreams blurred into his waking hours as he waited for his doom, which would ultimately be the consequences of the actions that he felt were beyond justified. He daydreamed about her, and they would bleed into real ones as he drifted into sleep. He often dozed accidentally, sitting upright, cocooned in his blankets, and he would wake to a change in light from the window, to bleak and familiar surroundings.

I should never have gone after the paladin, he thought. He often chastised himself with this notion. *I should have let them chase me.* Her face flashed in his mind. The memory was warped and fuzzy; a moment of reflection after they had awoken together. He drank in the sight of her, smiling as they shook the sleep from their eyes. The memory was almost gone and was now associated with pain and guilt. It hurt more than it comforted, and he found himself seething after he remembered.

Edgar knew that eventually his time would come. They would come for him and carry him away to face the emperor's justice. The difficult part for him was knowing how much time had passed.

He was fed twice a day, presumably in the morning and the evening. This was still difficult to ascertain, as the overcast sky and bright moons of Harbor made night almost as luminous as day. He counted the meals as meticulously as he was able, and came up with a count of forty-seven days.

At any moment, he knew, they would retrieve him. He hoped they would put him to death. Hopefully the Greater could grant him a kind of mercy that he was bereft of in his waking life.

He heard footsteps in the hall outside of his cell. *It can't be mealtime already... Or can it?* He listened intently as the sound grew louder. *Two men, they're coming this way. This is it. Resolution, absolution, relief.* He breathed deeply and rose from his bunk, laying the blanket neatly upon it. Edgar closed his eyes as he stood. His hand shook and tears welled, seeping through the pursed lids.

The clicks of boots against hard stone grew louder still, and it seemed to him to be deafening, impossibly thunderous, and still they came closer. He released a ragged breath as he was surrounded by this clamor bouncing off the walls and floor.

Then they stopped. At the peak of their volume they halted, and the lack of sound left a vacuum that stole the strength of his remaining limbs. He was uncertain of how long he would be able to support his weight once his legs began to shake.

A lonely beep came from the door, followed by a harsh click of the lock. Light poured in from the hall as the door creaked open. A silhouetted figure stood in the doorway, tall and broad.

"Edgar Thrawl," the man stated flatly. The voice was familiar.

"Yes?" Edgar croaked. The man signaled to another in the hall. "Is it time? Judgement?"

Two men entered the room, and Edgar could see them more clearly. The one that spoke, he had learned after the man escorted him off the Persistence, was Rohan Avery. Edgar's eyes widened in fear when he recognized the other paladin - the young man he had tried to ambush on Argon, right before they took his arm. Intimidated, he stepped back on shaky feet.

"You remember me, Edgar?" the young one asked. Edgar could only nod his head timidly. "Good. My name is Simon. Tell us about Evelesce."